LIVING THROUGH THE WAR IN BURMA

Boyhood Trials Shape the Chindit

TROPHY D'SOUZA

Copyright © 2021 by Trophy D'Souza

All rights reserved. No part of this publication may be reproduced, distributed, or transmitted in any form or by any means, including photocopying, recording, or other electronic or mechanical methods, without the prior written permission of the publisher, except in the case brief quotations embodied in critical reviews and other noncommercial uses permitted by copyright law.

ISBN: 978-1-63945-144-9 (Paperback)
       978-1-63945-145-6 (E-book)

The views expressed in this book are solely those of the author and do not necessarily reflect the views of the publisher, and the publisher hereby disclaims any responsibility for them.

Writers' Branding
1800-608-6550
www.writersbranding.com
orders@writersbranding.com

DECLARATION

The book records the experiences of Charles Stephenson in his early days and in the War. The facts and the interpretations of World War II situations are entirely those of Charles, as he has seen and experienced them. There is no intention either by Charles, or by the Author/Editor who has written the book for Charles, to misrepresent truth or history. The book highlights the struggles of an individual who came through against heavy odds, both in his early days as well as in the War. This publication is one of the many books of the Author to motivate, to inspire, to resolve and to empathize. There is no desire to cast aspersions at individuals or organizations. No beliefs have been challenged and there is no deliberate or subtle attempt to depreciate generally accepted values. All the writing is creative and original and there is no intention to plagiarize published work or to infringe copyright laws.

DEDICATION

Charles dedicates this book
to his Parents
who gave him life;
to his wife Daphne
who helped him appreciate
the great values in life.

This book is also dedicated to
Friends and Relatives
who have stood by him through
difficult times in his life.

The book is intended to record
the heroism and the skills
of all the CHINDITS
who fought in the War, and
especially the comradeship of those
who shared hardship and War with him.

This book is especially meant
to thank God and Virgin Mary
for inspiring and sustaining him
when he needed solace and support.

FOREWORD

Burma was a focal point in the War where the forces of the free world combined to curb the ambitions of the Axis Powers, especially of Japan in the Far East, as this book details. Charles takes us through a journey of fascinating accounts of his early life and of breath-taking experiences as a Chindit that also give reasonable coverage of the part played by Burma and the combined forces of the British Army in World War II. The Author has gone to great lengths to get Charles to tell his own story with all the passion of a war-veteran, eager to pass on historic realities to a world today that needs to know the truth.
— *FRG -Writer, Sociologist*

CONTENTS

Declaration	iii
Dedication	v
Foreword	vii
Chapter 1 Living life carefree in 'easy lane'	3
Chapter 2 Thriving in the land of opportunity	13
Chapter 3 Facing problems of learning and School	19
Chapter 4 Learning difficulties and slow growth	25
Chapter 5 Disappointing progress and failure	29
Chapter 6 Checking out new horizons and avenues	35
Chapter 7 Keeping close to home and friends	41
Chapter 8 Going for fresh challenges and avenues	47
Chapter 9 Training Schedules and adventure	55
Chapter 10 Getting deeper into war mode	59
Chapter 11 Evacuating positions and retreat	65
Chapter 12 Walking fears and Death Valley	71
Chapter 13 Relaxing in friendly territory	77
Chapter 14 Travelling hassles --ordinary style	81
Chapter 15 Training for intelligence and skills	89
Chapter 16 Invading with stealth and air power	97
Chapter 17 Facing danger in War mode	107
Chapter 18 Fighting intensely in war mode	111
Chapter 19 Experiencing new schedules in war mode	115
Chapter 20 Fighting to regain lost ground	121
Chapter 21 Coping with routines of war and rest	131
Chapter 22 Facing the moment of truth	137

Chapter 23 Seeing the softer side of war	143
Chapter 24 Dealing with the surrender	147
Chapter 25 Coping with new experiences	155
Chapter 26 Starting life again –new avenues	161
The Author	173
Guidance for Readers and Acknowledgements	175
GLOSSARY and NOTES	177
Map 1 – Burma – The Country	192

Living through the War in Burma
Boyhood Trials Shape The Chindit

Chapter 1

Living life carefree in 'easy lane'

'Charlie,' my Mum called. 'Come in now...it's getting late.'

It was really only 5 on that winter evening but as the sun was setting and as darkness crept in a lot earlier than in summer, Mum, motherly as ever, wanted me in, safe at home. I hadn't noticed at the time but my Mum seemed closer to me than to my other siblings. I can't really explain why but it was probably because, in spite of my silly pranks, I was always willing to do her errands or to help with her chores. She sometimes took me with her when she went shopping or when she had to go to the Doctor's. In later years this bond grew almost imperceptibly and it was perhaps the tonic that kept me going even during difficult times in the War. I often seemed to hear her caring voice warn me of impending danger or caution me if I tried to take too many risks.

I didn't see much of my Dad when we were growing up. He was busy at his work but he did provide for the family. Apart from that, as far as we can remember, he hardly did anything particularly noteworthy that helped nurture us as growing-up children. But Mum was there for us in those early days: from putting plasters on our little injuries to cooking our favourite dishes.

'Hurry along now,' Mum added a few moments later. 'And do look smart.'

'What's the hurry?' I asked. 'It's not supper time, is it? I just want to run around for a bit longer.'

'Some of our friends are coming over,' said Mum. 'You've also got a few things to do before they come.'

'Is Becky or Tiny coming?' I asked.

I never really wanted my Mum to call out a second time. Even though she was kind and loving a repeated call often meant a stern look I didn't want to face or perhaps a bit of a spank I didn't like getting. Of course I responded and I was back in not just trying to freshen up but also helping my Mum tidy up the sitting room as well. I always went along with what Mum wanted, and in my own little way, in spite of my clumsy and crazy habits, helped out with whatever Mum needed to do. I couldn't help noticing, even at that young age, that Mum spent hours caring for us all. It certainly helped build a bond that kept me linked to her and to the family.

As a family we were also part of a large group of friends of Anglo-Burmese° and Anglo-Indian° families around us. We met quite often to celebrate success or to share unpleasant outcomes. Everyone also helped out at parties and occasions. Then there were picnics, anniversaries and birthdays where everyone felt welcome and included as in a family. There were no formalities. We were also in and out of each other's houses as though our neighbours' homes were just extensions or other rooms in our own house.

The women often did more than just keep checking on each other's cooking or fashions, or curtains perhaps. They were always at hand to do some baby-sitting, emergency sewing or casual cooking. The men too were there always around if some heavy-duty work was required. Otherwise they were there comparing notes on the usual trivialities that men tend to discuss, especially over a drink.

For us young boys, the teenage girls, who were quite stunning, were really the attraction. The girls usually stayed bunched together as it gave them some common ground to keep a watch on their boy heroes while still staying quite protected in their homes. They were cute, beautiful and, I dare say, a lot more intelligent than most of us boys. I liked hanging out with some of them whenever the opportunity presented itself. They seemed to have had a somewhat more balanced outlook on life and situations. I certainly benefited from being with them though I feel they were as eager to be with us boys as we were to be close to them. In the bargain, I think, one or two of them got to like me.

'Does it matter?' Mum wanted to know. 'Just freshen up and look smart,' the usual standard advice most Anglo° parents were always ready with. Perhaps it did matter to me. It did matter too that every Anglo boy or girl, especially those in their teens, looked smart and presentable, almost like their British counterparts. It was as if the local population had set those standards for them.

Anglo-Burmese and Anglo-Indians even if they were in a minority in a largely Burman° population yet played a significant role in the way they may have affected the broader culture and society of the day. The Anglos it would seem worked closer to the masters and colonizers of the day, the British, than did the wider population.

The British, crafty planners as they were, knew how to assess places and people for their own purposes. When they moved into Burma they believed they had hit the jackpot in establishing themselves in this fascinating tropical paradise verdant with forests, sprawling with rice plantations, impressive with pagodas° and welcoming with friendly people.

When focusing their objectives, the British, correctly assumed that the English-speaking Anglos would be some of the ideal partners they needed in their plans to build an empire. They had sussed out that the Anglo-Burmese and the Anglo-Indians would be able to blend culture with development and use their sense of adventure and their flair for innovation and adaptation to temper and channel British interests into more achievable goals.

Whatever the rationale the British let some talented individuals in these groups take the lead when they were not too confident of projections in their plans. This gave the Anglos a certain licence to live their lives almost in the way they chose, sometimes aligning themselves with the colonizers, as in using the club privileges of the British, and at other times adapting to cultural demands of the wider population when it came to ethnic involvement in festivals or traditions.

Living life to the full
All I remember is that we lived our lives quite freely, neither harassed by the colonizers nor cautioned by the traditionalists. As growing up men and women, we too, boys and girls, felt almost no inhibitions to move around quite freely in a world

we believed was ours to enjoy and to build. Besides that, of course it would seem that generally Anglos always seem to exude a certain zest for life in spite of financial constraints or social inhibitions.

The typical Anglos, while always being law-abiding and totally committed to their jobs and to their communities, have never been too concerned about the pressures of daily living or too overwhelmed by how the laws of the land could affect them. Anglos seem to have this desire to make the best of life. It is perhaps this spirit that lets them live their lives freely and openly, almost never afraid of challenges or controversy, or perhaps even if somewhat unaware of outcomes. This is what possibly makes them great friends, good neighbours, reliable employees and loyal citizens.

Burmese society however, not unlike many people in the 'East', was somewhat conservative when it came to dealings with girls and women. This however did not affect the way the children of the Anglos mixed in social circles in Burma.

I'm not sure whether it was the teen-factor in me or the Anglo-brand but I certainly had an eye for girls even at that young age. I for one believed that being presentable or dressing up certainly mattered. Becky, one of the girls in the mix, was the cute one, just about my age, of the Saxty family, who lived a few doors away. Tiny, was not really tiny. She was Tiny Rainford who lived on the next street. She too was cute in her own way, and perhaps one I felt a little more attached to, as she often shared a few of her secrets about her teenage crushes. This really meant that I had made it on to her list of favourites. So, it did matter how I dressed up (even at that tender age of 12) and what 'first look' impression I gave.

Trophy D'Souza

Becky was more interested in holding my hand and wasn't really that particular about how I turned out. Tiny had inherited some of her dad's eyes for precision. He was an army man and was perhaps quite like Captain Von Trapp in the film, *The Sound of Music*, one for order and proper behaviour. I was really a little closer to her and couldn't afford to miss her slightest move or suggestion. There was no way I could get my Mum to attempt to understand that important part of 'growing-up etiquette', at least not in those somewhat 'conservative' days in the fifties when elders were as far from teenage realities as the moon is from the earth.

Meeting up or visiting was quite a regular chore especially at what was our weekend: Saturday and Sunday. We were a bunch of close-knit families –all Anglo-Burmese, living in the middle of a much wider group of Burmese people in a quaint little village, Thazi°, in central Burma. Thazi, like other places where Anglos lived especially, took on the colourful and carefree life enjoyed in many parts of Burma. The houses built of teak had roofs either thatched or of tin, with shops taking up spaces often alongside homes. Nature blended well into these houses as the flowering creepers made the homes look truly beautiful, really charming and very picturesque.

There were so many children playing or moving around and yet every little group seemed to be enjoying its own fun and games. These happy scenes perhaps did not reflect the struggles their elders and their parents had to cope with in bringing them up. The children needed no invitation to enjoy themselves even if there weren't so many open spaces to play in, at least not in the vicinity. There wasn't any real heavy traffic those days and children found it convenient to play on the roads. The boys generally kicked a ball around or tried to play rounders with used tennis balls, while the girls just bunched around in little groups talking about their little nothings or just enjoying their hopscotch. The girls looked pretty in their htameins° while the little boys were always a bit ragged but not really untidy. While playing on the roads the children just had to be a little careful about the clumsy bullock-carts (actually driven by buffaloes) that swayed unsteadily from side to side while their drivers, with their kamout° hats (made of leaves, and somewhat pointed), seemed asleep, almost unconcerned about where the buffaloes were taking them!

Exciting living for teenagers
Soon Thazi rose in importance. When the railway arrived the village became a little town with a steady growth in population, mainly with railway workers of course. Thazi moved up a notch and became a junction where four lines of railway met. To the south was Rangoon, the capital of Burma, to the east was Kalaw° and Toungyi° (which also had a small landing strip), to the west was Myingyan°, and to the north was Mandalay° –another of the larger and more important towns of Burma. Today Thazi is still a railway junction which people use to travel from Bagan° or Inle Lake°, both populated rural areas.

For me as a little child Thazi was heaven: I had such a great choice of playmates, especially those of the families we knew: the Saxtys and their 13 children, the Rainfords and their 7 children, the Rodricks and their 6 children, the Campbells and their 5, and many others.

My early pre-teen years were really exciting and memorable. Of course we did school, but the real joy of living was the fun we had together: the bunch of us --gangs of little boys up to all sorts of pranks and adventures. I loved the outdoors and spent many hours shooting birds with a catapult, and I dare say I was as good and accurate as David° who knocked down the great Goliath. I also knew how to trap sparrows and pigeons by luring the birds to a basket trap attached to a 'remote control' string.

My Mum was always mighty pleased with any catch I made and would really delight the family by cleaning and cooking the birds that very day, and of course enriching our lunch snacks or the evening meals. It is interesting that even today birds, like sparrows and pigeons, are still part of the popular cuisine in these areas, sold as snacks at the railway stations or as delicacies at the local restaurants. But soon this outdoor life --free from harsh rules and regulations, and filled with inventive play and adventure, packed with freedom in running, climbing, skipping, jumping and playing all day-- would come to an end.

The picture of a laidback Thazi was probably that of an almost 'lotus-eater-like'° situation in Burma as compared to the active progress that one of its neighbours, India, was making. Yet in spite of that slow development Burma was actually making steady progress, perhaps more than at almost any other time in its history. The Burmese were enterprising and hard-working, and they focused on their crops and their little businesses. In fact other colonizers thought the British, who were in control of both India and Burma, were fortunate to have Burma and often referred to it as 'the rice bowl of South East Asia.'

Yet it was the Indians only, probably because they were somewhat more prosperous, who enjoyed the privilege of travelling hassle free between India and Burma. The British saw trade in the process and began developing the railways. They saw the possibility of recruiting Indian expertise and labour to build the railways. A rigorous programme of building began in the late 1880s, and the line from Rangoon near the sea to Mandalay in the northern heartland was completed by 1889.

It was another 10 years before the line further north to Myitkyina°, a total of 2600 km was completed. This was a vital link to the air-strip at Myitkyina which later proved to be a life-line in the air-rescue operations of both army and civilian personnel from Burma to India. But the need for labour also offered employment, especially for adventurous Indians who believed they could make their fortunes in this developing land of plenty. My grandfather took a chance and brought his whole family from India to settle in Burma, the land that seemed to offer prospects for a better life.

Chapter 2

Thriving in the land of opportunity

When my father, George William, was brought over to Burma by my grandfather he was still a little boy. My Dad had no idea when he was taken away from Vizagapatam in south-eastern India, where he was born, that life would change for him before he really began growing up. At twelve he joined the Burma Railways as an odd-job boy in the railway locomotive sheds. People believed that the railways always offered stable and secure employment. This naturally encouraged those who were unemployed to try every possible way to get into the railways. Dedication and constancy were highly-valued qualities that assured progress especially on the railways. My Dad stayed committed to his work and consequently moved on from Fireman to Shunter-Driver and then to Driver. That brought him stability and a steady income, which proved absolutely vital in keeping our little family going.

The social club, which Dad was allowed to be part of, brought my father in touch with another family, the Coopers. Mr Cooper was an Englishman married to Daw Thein, who was Burmese. So, their daughter, who married my Dad, was of Anglo-Burmese descent. Together my parents had eight children: five girls (Georgia, Madge, Beryl, Clare, Maureen) and three boys (Charles, Ashley, Noel). I was the third child, the first boy of the family. I was born in a little place called Pyuntaza°. His work on the railways allowed my Dad to travel but it was not always convenient for the family to move around to the places where he was posted. There was always something that didn't suit: either the climate wasn't to our liking, or school facilities were not available.

Soon after I was born we were transferred to a beautiful hill station situated at the edge of the Shan Plateau in the North East of Burma, Maymyo°. This unique town had a typical British setting, cool and mountainous almost like central UK, or perhaps like one of the hill stations in India like Darjeeling. It was a town built and developed for the benefit of the diplomatic personnel who could use it as a resort or a holiday retreat, when temperatures in their work places like Rangoon became too clammy or unbearable. Dad was posted here as a driver on the ghat section of the railways. Mum however found Maymyo too cold so Dad applied for a transfer to a warmer climate. That is how we landed at this junction station, Thazi, which seemed to have the ideal climate that Mum and the family liked.

Learning systems in Burma

Most of the Burmese were literate in their language, as every village had a *Phongyi Kyaung* (a Buddhist Monk school). These schools were free and open to everyone but were compulsory too. The Buddhist monks believed in discipline and students had to toe the line. Yet somehow, almost unbelievably, they knew how to foster a happy environment at school. The Burmese valued education and parents ensured that their children attended school every day. So the *Phongyi Kyaung* student very rarely played truant. Unfortunately the curriculum was very restricted. The monks only taught Buddhist philosophy, Burmese, Pali° (the language of Buddhism), and numeracy (basic arithmetic and calculations). The Burmese villagers, whose only models were the Buddhist monks, were more than content with the knowledge they were given.

There was however a sting in the tail. The monks provided the ideals but the paymasters were really the British. In order to get into their ranks it was essential to be good at English. Most of the Indians, the Chinese and the Anglo-Burmese took the hint and enrolled in Government English High Schools or Mission Schools run by the American Baptist°, the Anglican°, the Methodist° or the Catholic° or Christian organizations.

Some of the smarter ones among the tribal groups, like the Karens° and the Arkanese°, followed suit to get their children into these schools as well. All these schools promoted English and used English as the medium of instruction. Students learned English, English Literature, English History, Geography, Mathematics and the Sciences. They also had to learn either Higher Burmese or Lower Burmese, which appears to have been the deciding factor in job selection especially for Government jobs. Those of course with Higher Burmese got jobs higher up in the inner circles of Government administration or high-profile private institutions, while those who only managed Lower Burmese were in the outer circles of positions of authority and control. They might, for example, have managed a job as a bank clerk but not as a bank manager.

Trophy D'Souza

Knowing English makes the difference

Those who graduated from the 'English' education schools received a very good education and got top positions in the work force. Unfortunately these 'English' schools did very little to teach their students the culture, history and literature of the country. Many Anglo-Burmese especially, [possibly those who took up Lower (Basic) Burmese] grew up unaware of the Burmese way of life. Some of them could not speak Burmese at all.

Suddenly a new consciousness arose among the powerful group of Buddhist thinkers (many of whom were monks), who still exerted a fair amount of influence over even the British. They had their roots in the Burman sector of the population, who were supposed to be the real descendants of Burma. They feared that the Buddhism embraced from the time of Anawartha° (one of the main rulers who promoted Buddhist thought and belief) would trickle down to a spiritual vacuum. It created needless panic in these 'thinking circles'. Their thinking was aired through the local press and the occasional interviews on radio.

There was another problem too. Burma under British rule was really a part of greater India for them. The average Burman feared that his values and beliefs would get lost and that the Burmese people would eventually get absorbed into the greater population of India and would become Indian and lose their identity as Burmese. This urged some of the more aggressive Burmese thinkers to demand from the British that Burma be separated from India. The thrust of the movement came from students at Rangoon University. Aung San°, the father of Aung Sang Suu Kyi ° (the lady who got into politics, after many years of house arrest) also became active in politics.

He however crossed over to Japan and formed the Burma Liberation Army to fight the British. The British didn't quite know what to make of him. Later paradoxically Aung San became recognized as the 'Father of the Nation'.

Students went on strike after strike and so education and teaching at university got disrupted. With universities not being able to award qualifications to those with High School Diplomas got priority in the job market. A Tenth Standard pass could get one a clerical position, while even a Seventh Standard pass, with an English-Pass certificate, could help in social mobility, where even a 'coolie'(or porter) or farm-worker could get a respectable position. Apparently this must have affected the quality of administrative government and that of general business management.

Chapter 3

Facing problems of learning and School

Mum and Dad were apparently not pleased with what the Burmese school offered and assumed that there was no possibility of anything changing for education in the foreseeable future. Thazi was just a small town that wasn't really developing. Many railway towns often do not appear to have much scope for development or expansion. That, my parents assumed, would naturally stunt our educational development. It gave them serious cause for concern.

Mum and Dad acted quickly and sent me to a boarding school in Mandalay when I was really young. It was actually a convent school run by Nuns, which was really meant for girls. Only the kindergarten had co-education but only for those students who had siblings in school. Once the boys passed that stage and were eligible to attend the First Standard, they were transferred to the all-boys section the parents chose. My early school years were spent at Catholic boarding schools. I hated boarding life, and from here onwards events in my life took a downward spiral.

Trophy D'Souza

Going through Boarding School

I was just four and a half years of age when I had to experience what it was to be a boarder. The first day at school is etched in my memory, never to be forgotten. I was not very sure of what to expect.

I remember clinging to my mother, not wanting to let go, and the Nun putting her arms around me while telling my Mum, 'Mrs. Stephenson, don't worry. We'll look after him.'

This was an alien environment with large buildings surrounding the open area in the middle. The high walls that enclosed the rest of the area without buildings seemed to make the place look more like a prison than a home. What was more painful was that my sisters, in the same school, were not anywhere close by. They were on the other side of the convent. All I could wish for at that moment was to be at home --a place where I felt comfortable, safe and secure. I loved my Mum. I wanted to be with her more than anything in the world but try as I did to struggle out of the Nun's strong grip, I failed. All I could do was to watch Mum enter the 'gharry' (horse carriage --a mini version of a stage-coach) and the last thing I remember was the carriage fading out of sight as it rolled on towards the train station not too far away.

In my memory there was only the picture of my beloved mother back home in Thazi, without me. The only way I could give expression to my feelings and let off my grief was to cry. As soon as the gharry turned the corner the Nun, who had been so loving only minutes earlier, squeezed my ears and twisted them, saying, 'Come on now, stop crying.' I never knew Nuns could be so hard-hearted!

The pain was so intense that I was shocked into silence. The Nun's method worked for her: she managed to control a screaming child. But for me 'the reign of terror' had just begun. For the next few days all I could think of was my Mum and Thazi. I cried when the Nuns were not looking for fear that I would have my ears twisted. As the days passed I eventually got to accept the situation. I felt very unhappy. What was I to do in this place? Where would I hide? When could I go home?

The school was structured into three types of boarders: the first class boarders were the elite of society. Their parents paid the full fees and so they were pampered. They had their own dormitories and dining rooms. The second class boarders paid a percentage of the full fees. The third class boarders were the orphans or those whose parents could not afford to pay any fees. I was a second class boarder. A fair bit of discrimination definitely existed regarding the treatment towards the boarders by the Nuns, something that had to be endured and accepted in those days. All I remember of course is that I survived in that pretty unfriendly environment.

Boarders had no choice of menu. At meal time you ate what was put before you. It was not like home where I could be fussy with mum if I did not want to eat what was served. At home I did not eat the fat on meat, nor did I eat chicken skin. In fact I refused to eat anything that looked slimy. I remember one day at dinner time meat full of fat was placed before me. I just could not eat the fat so I pushed it aside. Each time I did this the Nun supervising, to see that we did not waste any food, came from behind me and said, 'Eat it,' and hit me on the head. I put the fatty meat in my mouth but I just could not swallow it. So I took the meat out again. Once again I was told to 'eat it'. This went on and on, until finally out of fear I swallowed the piece of fat. The whole saga of the dining room incident went on and on, day after day, until finally of course the school holidays came. I was mighty relieved to go home when the school term ended.

When the holidays came to an end, the trauma of leaving home began again. The crying appeals of 'I do not want to go to boarding school' fell on deaf ears. My sisters were housed on the girls' side, which was about four hundred yards from where we boys were. Strangely our toilets were on the girls' side.

Every Saturday morning we little fellows lined up in front of a Nun standing very austere with a bottle of castor oil in her hand, which she poured into a large spoon and forced down our throats. Anyone who has had to taste castor oil will know how disgusting it is. After this we were given a portion of fried-battered onions or something similar to eat because our parents were paying fees. Unfortunately the third class boarders did not get anything to eat after the dreaded castor gulp and suffered the unpleasant taste of castor oil lingering on their palates for several hours, because their parents did not pay fees. I felt sorry for my third class boarder friends and shared my fried-battered onions with some of them.

On one Saturday after the castor oil routine my stomach rumbled with wind and then ached terribly. I ran towards the toilets on the girls' side. Before I could reach my destination the inevitable happened. I had runny faeces all down my leg. I stood there crying. One of the girls who noticed my predicament called out to my sisters to attend to me, but when they arrived the smell was so disgusting that they did not want to clean me. The Nuns were then informed and arrangements were made for the nanny to clean me up. It was a terrible and embarrassing experience. More than the fact that I was in shock and in pain was the terrifying reality that I could be in serious trouble.

In the classroom I faced another problem. I am naturally left-handed and felt comfortable writing with this hand. The rule at the time was that every student had to write with the right-hand. In those days the teachers perceived being left-handed as an error of nature or a disability. One of the reasons for the dismal belief was that being left-handed ('left' in Latin was 'sinister') was an evil omen. Being left-handed was considered clumsy, awkward, unlucky, insincere, sinister and even malicious. Some educators and teachers actually believed that to be left-handed was to be associated with the devil.

Therefore we were advised that a good Christian student should not write with the left-hand. Whenever I attempted to follow my natural ability, a teacher promptly gave me a smack on the knuckles with a ruler. Nothing seemed to work for me. It seemed that whatever I did at school was wrong. My confidence was shattered. I was very unhappy in this environment. As a result I could not learn and never passed an exam. Yes, we had to sit for examinations even at that very young age. Unfortunately I also got no sympathy from Mum or Dad. All they could say was,

Chapter 4

Learning difficulties and slow growth

The time finally arrived for me to attend an all-boys school. Arrangements were made for me to attend St. Paul's High School in Rangoon run by the De La Salle° Brothers°. The school had a very good reputation for academic achievement and was known as one of the top schools in Burma. However for someone with learning difficulties this was not a correct choice.

When I sat in the First Standard class on the first day of school, I did not have a clue about what was being said or taught by the teacher. It was double Dutch to me. In those days if we did not understand something in the class we tried to use different phrases to express our problems like 'donno Sir', 'can't get it Sir', 'not clear Sir', 'can't follow, Sir'. Very seldom the teachers, who were generally Brothers, stopped the lesson or cared to explain details to thick-heads like me. The standard at St. Paul's was a lot higher than that of the convent school in Mandalay. The curriculum was certainly not designed for dullards like me. So for the most part I sat in the class confused and quite naturally very unhappy, and quite insecure really.

Trophy D'Souza

As the days passed all the answers to my class work or tests were wrong and there was no one to help me correct my errors. My confidence in my ability to learn was rock bottom. I began to fear that if I failed the grades I would really be in serious trouble. Till today I can't ever forget the fear instilled by the Brothers who regularly and mercilessly flogged the children who could not learn. I did not know how to tell the Brothers that I just was not capable of learning. How was I to explain to the Brothers that I had a learning impediment? How on earth could I dare explain to them that flogging would not increase the power of the brain cells? In fact flogging only blocked my ability to learn.

Teaching --the non-caring way

Could the Brothers not have understood that perhaps some tender loving care may have worked to improve my condition? Why was I always made to feel there was something wrong with me? If my teachers had stopped their relentless oppressive methods even for a moment to find out who I was they might have discovered that down there at the bottom, at heart, I was a good fellow: a crack shot with my catapult and a real sweetheart. They would have found out that I may have been slightly mischievous but that I was a normal lively boy, and that there was nothing really wrong with me. I just needed some 'support' in my learning schedule. That word did not exist in the Brothers' thinking or vocabulary.

I never passed an exam to be promoted to the next class. Year after year Mum pleaded with the Brothers to give me another chance, 'Brother, please push him up.' I can't really explain how but I was pushed up to the next Standard. This annual ritual continued year after year. Mum's pleading saw me through to the Fourth Standard. Eventually Mum backed down and agreed, 'This school is not right for you.'

After a discussion with Dad, I was sent to another Brothers' school, St. John's in Kalaw.

What the teachers failed to understand was that I did not have a strong grounding of the basic concepts of learning and needed some sort of remedial programme to achieve. But in those days I do not think remedial classes existed. You sat in one Standard until you passed. As I was never able to grasp the rudiments of English and Mathematics once again, I was faced with the same situation. I was rapped and beaten whenever I failed.

Learning --the Brothers' way

This School was not working for me either and still there was no one to understand that perhaps I could have been dyslexic and that possibly I needed individual attention to grasp the basics taught. Once again my parents felt the school was not doing me any good. So, after much deliberation they decided that instead of boarding school, I would live with an aunt in Rangoon and attend St John's Diocesan Boys School, on Pagoda Road, in Rangoon, as a Day Scholar. This was another school of high academic standards, with an excellent achievement record in sport as well. The school was not nearby. I had to cycle two miles to the train station and from there catch the train to attend St John's.

After school, when back at my aunt's place, she dutifully tried to teach me my lessons. But for some reason I had a mental block. Try as hard as I could I just could not grasp the concepts. She could not understand what was holding me back, neither did I. The results always showed: Spelling –zero, Maths –zero, Burmese –zero, English –zero. Everything I attempted resulted in failure. It seemed the examination papers never seemed to ask what I did know and could do. The papers always contained something I did not understand. After just one year my aunt gave up. Although my aunt was a helpful lady I noticed she served the same brinjal (okra) curry for me day after day. After the harsh boarding school experience I had learned to eat what was served without any complaint. This was far better than what the Prodigal Son° in the Bible (Gospel°) story had no choice but to eat, while trying to survive away from the love and care of his father.

Chapter 5

Disappointing progress and failure

My situation in life at this point was perhaps not very different to those soldiers who went headlong to their deaths in the '*Charge of the Light Brigade*', in Tennyson's° poem. Maybe they did know that they would die. In my case I knew that I was going to get punished, to get beaten and to get humiliated no matter what I did. Yet I knew I had no choice. My fate too was just 'to do and die'! I knew I was hopeless and useless and I was going to get misunderstood and punished just for being what I was. I was usually not at fault most of the time and yet I knew that I would get punished. My gut instincts goaded me on to keep at the routines and schedules that came my way. I was led on almost headlong and somewhat blindly into all sorts of situations, the way the 'Light Brigade' went for the 'Charge'!

At this point in my life I also knew that I was certainly a headache for my Mum and Dad. I lasted only a year at St John's. I was then placed into St Peter's, Mandalay, another Brothers' school, again as a boarder. Once again I started in the Fourth Standard and had to repeat the Grade until I passed.

Trophy D'Souza

I had Mr. Sweeny teaching me, with no success of course, so I had to repeat the year again in Mrs. Rodgers' class.

There was no sympathy from Mum and Dad either. All they said was, 'You're stupid. That's all you are. You're no good at anything.'

Coping with failure and misfortune
When I look back today I just don't know how I bore the brunt of being put down at school and at home. I'm not sure if, besides being dull, I was also really thick-skinned or maybe I had developed a sort of built-in resilience to cope with failure and misfortune. Or maybe, just maybe somewhere deep down in me, unlearned as I was, there was some spark of self-belief or perhaps the human-superhuman element that Bernard Shaw° speaks of and tries to stand up for in his plays, Man and Superman and Saint Joan. Or maybe perhaps it was a sort of survival toughness (that Darwin° writes of) that not even my parents could believe their genes had produced.

The Brothers, however, who had taught hundreds of young people over the years, couldn't but conclude that deep down I was lazy or perhaps unsuitable material for education. I am assuming that the Brothers must have had their training and their updating. In those days however they were the Gods of Education and no one ever questioned their systems or their traditions. They had produced heroes, stalwarts and champions. Who was I, the dull, lazy brat in that great mix? I was probably a one-in-a-million misfit, not worth remembering. Anyway, try as hard as I could, I couldn't see success anywhere in my sights. Eventually I just got resigned to the idea that there would never be any academic success for me. I began to convince myself that I was really stupid.

So, quite naturally I grew up feeling very disappointed with life. There were moments when I went into moods of deep sadness and depression. As time went by the emotions of the past hurt I had received during my younger days began to flood my memory and they began to blank out any feelings of tenderness and sensitivity inside me. There were other days when I began to feel very sorry for myself and to spend hours in self-pity. There were also moments, when I was alone and by myself, when I just burst into tears of hopelessness and frustration.

This feeling of failure was painful to bear and unpleasant to accept. Sometimes it brought me close to despair. I used to wonder why my parents brought me into this world at all. I compared myself with my mates and was quite alarmed to find out how I had come so far without any real learning, and sadly without any real friends as well.

My teachers seemed to have given up on me and many of my classmates thought I was the 'classified dunce' of the class: the sort of 'class clown'. For the records anyway that indeed was the sort of 'final progress report' of my life at school. It was not a good start in life but perhaps that was the only road ahead for me: plodding along almost like a headless chicken. I was facing a reality that I had somehow got accustomed to and had endured over the years. I was in some ways living in a sort of a horror movie that was going past me regularly and relentlessly, almost without any hope of light at the end of the tunnel.

Trophy D'Souza

Persisting to no purpose

Yet there was some persistence about the way life rolled on for me. I can't explain how I could put on enough cheer to keep up with the rigours of the school routine. Day after day I dutifully sat in the study hall almost idly, staring at my books and tasks. We were not allowed to talk or ask questions while at study. There was in actual fact no one to assist us with the homework. I sat at my desk, pulled out my books, took out the sheet for homework and I just did not know how to proceed. I tried to do some figures in Mathematics. I then tried to read and answer the questions in English or Geography or History, only to find the next day in class that I had got them all wrong. Sometimes I just could not do any bits of the home work at all. In class I was regularly flogged by the teacher or the Brother-in-charge either because I couldn't do the home work or had got it all wrong.

The day the Brother Director paid the class a visit was doomsday for me. Everyone dutifully put their report cards on the desk at the side for the Director to see. Mine of course read 'Unsatisfactory' and that naturally meant public flogging. You were placed in the middle of the study hall in front of all the boys and received four to six sharp lashes with the cane. So frightened was I at times that I urinated in my pants. There were times when I could not sit down properly after that for days. The welts from the cane hits stood out like ridges on my thighs. In those days the junior students did not wear underpants. With no extra padding for the thin cotton shorts the pain was extremely painful and truly unbearable.

I could not help but cry in pain during the flogging and long after the beating. It was a no-win situation for me. Who could I ask for help with my lessons when we were not allowed to talk or ask questions? If I had been allowed to ask my fellow students in class for help it may have been a different story. That was out of the question.

In the playground too it was the survival of the fittest. Today I wish Charles Darwin° would have come round my school: he would have had abundant proof of his theories. If there was an argument with a fellow student, or someone set up a fight, the unfortunate person was rewarded with a flogging. A fair hearing or a chance to explain things was unheard of during the years I spent at school in all these institutions of Brothers. I often used to wonder if these Brothers had only really been trained in how to cane students. Was that perhaps part of the training that all teachers and educators went through?

All I know now is that I had little sympathy or respect for the Brothers when I finally left school. If you were the unlucky one to be called out in the middle of the dormitory it was further agony. Once again all the boys stood around looking wide-eyed from the side of their beds. The flogging seemed endless whether it was four or six cuts of the cane. You rubbed and rubbed your bottom but the pain lingered. All you could do was to bury your head in your pillow and cry yourself to sleep.

Punishing and caning serve no purpose
The Brothers in the schools were Irish or German. I found the German Brothers to be much harsher in their dealings when calling for discipline. That was the life at school in our days and we had no choice but to accept the way it was. Caning was part of the agenda in the life of the school child. The teachers

and Brothers seemed to have honed their skills in merciless caning more than in 'inclusive' teaching. For those who were rebellious or boisterous or indeed bullies, perhaps the cane did put them on the right track. But for children with learning difficulties, like me, it did more harm than good.

I will never stop wondering, even today, why those Brothers, those learned men, failed to understand that a child is always a child who needs understanding, especially when the fault he has or shows is no fault of his own. If this had happened today perhaps some of these teachers and Brothers could have been brought to justice. In those days authority was always right. One weakling Anglo-Burmese boy appearing on this rather hazy horizon (of pranks, mischief and unruly behaviour) was not going to signal the coming of the better times of summer (even if one swallow could). There was no hope even if one showed compensating skills by being accurate with the catapult in actually hitting a sparrow down! Academics mattered, and there was no aggregate of other skills (physical, social, intellectual, emotional) that could justify acceptance or achievement, or perhaps even the intention to improve or progress.

Chapter 6

Checking out new horizons and avenues

However, in spite of all that harsh period in my life, I did learn something very important at school. My learning ability may have diminished, but my spirituality increased. I learned how to pray with all my heart and with all my soul. I had great faith in Our Lady, (the Virgin Mary, the Mother of Jesus), and I always felt that it was by her grace that I had managed to survive the senseless floggings and the merciless beatings. My praying gave me inner strength and guided me through all those troubles and tribulations that life served up. I felt strengthened as a Christian, with Jesus Christ as my hero, my guide and my strength.

Back at home I felt happier as I had many playmates. We spent a lot of time outdoors, and enjoyed good home cooking. All this was great until the postman delivered the Report Card from school. Then all hell broke loose!

On that day, after Dad had come home from his trip, had had his bath, and then had come down the stairs for his dinner, it all happened. Mum would put the report card in front of him and then out came the 'shotgun', his belt! Then the relentless beating started not only on my buttocks but all over my body. Many a time I had welts and cuts on my hands and face as well. I tried to run to escape the 'gun-fire' but all in vain. Dad chased me and kept hitting me until his anger subsided and he ended up seemingly more tired than I was. That was the kind of Dad I had. It was an unbearably tough life: flogged at school and belted at home. As a young boy I dreaded the days my Dad came home, especially on Report day. It was not only the Report Card horror that I remember. There were so many other incidents too that I can recall, when I was on the wrong side of reason and understanding.

Enjoying outdoor life & activity

No matter what was happening to me, I always enjoyed my life at Thazi. My best mates lived here, and of course I had my catapult. I was a 'crack shot' so to speak. During the school holidays, on one of my catapult outings, I came across a large beehive about four feet in diameter, hanging high up on a very tall tree. It was a target for a mischievous boy's prank. I was tempted to try a shot and just could not resist the challenge. What was more intriguing was that I was very confident that I could out-run the bees after I'd hit the target. I backed away from the tree to take good aim but I must have miscalculated. I was not too close or too far but the excitement was high inside me. I moved back to a distance of sixty feet, which would have been the distance I needed to take good aim at the target. I loaded my catapult with a large rounded stone and pulled the rubber bands of the catapult until they could stretch no more and let the stone go. Whack! As the stone left the catapult I turned and ran.

Within seconds I could hear this great big 'buzz'. The swarm of bees was all over me, chasing me with stinging vengeance. I charged down the pathway as fast as my legs would carry me. I can't believe that I had the guts to turn around to check what had happened. All I could see was this massive black cloud of bees heading for me, surrounding me, enveloping me entirely. The bees were literally travelling supersonic as compared to my buffalo-cart speed. In seconds they were all over me: stinging me all over -my head, my arms, my legs, my face -just everywhere. I had nowhere to hide. I managed to crush a few with my feeble efforts. But the bees came at me wave after wave, as the relentless siege went on. They attacked me in groups, but with deadly precision. After one group had stung me they went off and the next group came on. I was just too dazed to realize what was happening. It was as if the 'bee armies' were avenged that they had taught a naughty boy a lesson.

I arrived home in agony and in tears. My head was swollen like a pumpkin. My arms and legs were wounded limbs that didn't seem to belong to me. For days Mum had to pull out the bee stings from my body. All that Mum said, in her sort of 'controlled temper' was, 'Serves you right, you mischievous brat.' I was fortunate that I was not allergic to bee stings and that the sting poisons hadn't harmed me really. Maybe the beatings at school had in a way toughened my body to attack. The bees of course had done their best but this 'thoroughbred' Anglo-Burmese warrior would live to fight many more intense battles!

Trophy D'Souza

Having a friend is a blessing

On another shooting expedition, my next-door neighbour's son, Clinton Rodrigues, who was very much younger to me, wanted to accompany me on one of my expeditions. I told him that this was a big boys' shooting spree and that he would not manage the trip. But he insisted on following me. We trekked a fair way out into the bush looking for birds. Clinton being a small fellow lagged behind. As we continued on I could get a strong smell of faeces. Sure enough there was a large trench, about fifteen feet long and four feet wide. There were quite a few waste pits covered with leaves that were full.

I shouted out a warning to Clinton, 'Be careful! There's shit on the right and shit on the left. You have to walk in between. Follow me.'

When I turned around again Clinton was no longer in sight. Then I saw his hand come up. I rushed there and grabbed his hand and hauled him out of the pit. It was not a pretty sight. There were lumps of faeces stuck to him and the stench was unbearable. Anyway, somehow we ran all the way home, with my little friend crying all the way. As we ran nearer to his home his mother heard us and came out to see what had happened. She gasped at her son's disgusting sight, quickly gave him a hot bath and after that a good dose of castor oil. In a sort of merciful way she left the spanking for later!

Clinton lives here in Perth (Australia), not far from me. Whenever we meet we laugh at the crazy times we had together as kids. We have known each other for seventy years and are still good friends. I received no medal for saving a life that day. I received no praise from my parents, or from his parents, but I gained a loyal friend for life. Friends do matter!

All I can remember on several occasions was my mother complaining to my father, 'Charlie climbed a tree today', or 'Charlie came home late for lunch' or 'Charlie went out on his own'. That's all that was needed to prompt my Dad. Out came his belt and what followed of course was endless beatings at home, and when progress at learning was bad or slow the inevitable whipping at school. No wonder I hated homework and my Dad coming home from work during my holidays.

Chapter 7

Keeping close to home and friends

The year I turned thirteen my Dad had a stroke. Half of his body, on the right-hand side, was paralysed. He never fully recovered from this physical impediment. In fact, after just about a year in Thazi, he was forced to retire, having done only around thirty years of service. He was given a 'good handshake' and his Provident Fund came in useful. Mum was wise and cautious and avoided any wasteful spending. We then moved to Rangoon, to the suburb, Malwagon°. The Management of the Railways were kind to us and allowed us to rent one of their railway quarters. We stayed in the flat on the first floor while another retired driver lived on the ground floor.

My Dad was out of hospital by then and looked pitiful as he dragged his right leg around the house. By then I had forgotten all the beatings he had given me. Deep down inside me I loved my parents and so I did all I could in his hour of need. I bathed and dressed him and took him for walks. I somehow felt proud to do something for my Dad. Maybe it was this spiritual belief I had that sustained me and at this point seemed to tell me that God would bless me if I cared

Trophy D'Souza

for him. If I remember correctly, the *10 Commandments*° say something about *'honouring your father and mother.'*

Saving pennies for the road

By now I was fourteen years old and in the Fifth Standard in St. Paul's, as a Day Scholar. Everyday I was given two *annas*° for lunch and six *pice*° for train fare, three for going and three for coming. Sometimes I used the train fare for a better lunch. I was a growing boy, and the two *annas* for lunch were not enough to buy more food to satisfy the hunger. With the train money all gone, in the evening I would have no choice but to take the long walk home along the railway tracks, to Rangoon station, past Pazaungdaung° and on to Malwagon. I did this quite often. I was tough enough to do without the train-ride but not the food. I think the walk helped keep me fit.

On one Saturday, one of the servants' wives, with just a sarong° on, was having a body wash in an empty kitchen downstairs in the servants' living quarters, just below where we lived. I happened to be passing by on my way back home which was upstairs, with all my catapults around my waist. I was fond of shooting birds and frying them and then of course eating them: doves, pigeons, sparrows. Not really thinking about what I was doing I walked right into the living quarters of the servant and began talking to her in quite a familiar way. Besides getting pretty garrulous, I began to get a bit smooth and perhaps a bit over the top. In those days there weren't any of the social distinctions that exist today and all the families, including the children, just got along pretty well, owners, masters and servants.

But on this occasion perhaps I was really attracted to the body of the woman, the wet sarong clinging to her body making her look very sexy. My teenage hormones got the better of me, and my imagination ran wild. The conversation soon began to build up and my heart began racing as my eyes just gorged on the scene. I could almost see her warm up towards me. I probably had some enticing talk to add to my endearing style. Yet, somehow from her 'watch tower', my Mum had noticed me coming home.

She then saw that I had suddenly disappeared into one of the servant's quarters and began imagining the trap that I was actually falling into. She wasted no time in stopping any nonsense that could have happened. She immediately yelled out to me from upstairs, with all the vehemence and anger only a troubled mother could muster, 'Come up, Charlie, NOW!' The call was so loud and demanding that it shook me back into reality. I noticed the tone of annoyance in her voice and needed no second call to reinforce the message.

More than just being angry she was probably upset to see her son eyeing a servant woman, a married woman, and (in the social eyes of the day) a low-caste woman. It would have been a disgrace to our family if I had even just tried to touch the woman. As soon as I entered my house my Mum had her whip ready. She hit me till I was blue and until she herself was exhausted. The cane actually broke on me. I was a strong teenager now and could take a beating but I was also very angry with the caning I kept getting. I was in my own way trying to bring in the reason and understanding argument, even if punishment was involved. Yes, I broke the remaining bits of cane to pieces for a start. In a weird kind of a way I think my mother seemed to get the message that beating and caning were not necessarily the best punishments for bad behaviour.

Chatting up --Burmese style
One day after taking Dad for a walk, I sat down for a chat with a friend, Charlie Walmsley. His father was also a train-driver. They lived in the middle of the railway housing block. We were sitting on the stairs of one of the buildings chatting when this petite Burmese girl selling *moke phet thoke°* --a sweet made of glutinous rice with a bit of jaggery (palm sugar) in the middle wrapped in a leaf and steamed-- came by

Charlie asked me, 'Have you got any money?'

'Yes,' I replied. 'I have a *rupee°* on me: a birthday present I received a while ago.'

Charlie continued, 'What about us getting some *moke phet thoke* to eat?'

I jumped at the idea, 'OK!'

The girl heard us. She was around 15 years old, just about the same age as we were. She put her basket full of this sweet down and said we could get two pieces for one *pice°*.

Four *pice* were equal to one *anna*', and sixteen *annas* made a *rupee*. I had 64 *pice*.

We bought two *pice* worth, which gave us two pieces each. We had barely eaten a morsel when the girl decided to move on with her sales. She had just about begun walking off when Charlie said, 'Oh! Come on, let's get another lot.'

We asked the girl to come back. In the mean time I looked at Charlie and thought, 'Why does he want to eat *moke phet thoke*?' Then it dawned on me, that every time she walked away he was enjoying the swaying of her hips. I then couldn't help thinking to myself, 'Oh! The little rascal!' She did have a lovely body and balancing the basket on her head while straightening her posture, added to the natural sway of her well-shaped hips.

As curious teenagers of course just watching the female body, especially if it was beautiful or buxom, gave us a lot of pleasure. It was something that we didn't talk about so much but as boys we all felt the same way about watching attractive women or girls pass by or do something on the street. That particular day we just targeted this teenage girl vendor. We called her back thirty two times. The girl went home happy. She had sold her whole basket of wares without having to walk the whole morning. We were left with a huge pile of *moke phet thoke*.

Was it worth it? Well! Charlie had his thrills and I was sick eating the sweet. We gave the rest of the *moke phet thoke* to our poor friends, the lower class Indians, the untouchables. Their mothers swept and cleaned our toilet bowls for us and emptied them into the latrine at the back, where the night cart came and took away the contents. Her sons Swamy, Noondegar, Mutu and Yankana were our good mates too.

Chapter 8

Going for fresh challenges and avenues

School soon got boring as I got into my teens. I hadn't picked up even a reasonable bit of academic knowledge. Yet, in spite of the rigors of the Brothers' training schedules and of their particular brand of education -weird though it seemed- I felt I had matured in other ways. In fact, almost by default the toughness that we developed because of the senseless punishments made us (at least me for one) into young men ready for a harsh world.

I thought I was ready for a challenge and that too away from school. But in our days there wasn't much on offer. In one of our lazy laidback chats one day Charlie Walmsley, almost as a careless remark said, 'You think we could join the army?'

It was as if a comet had whizzed past us. 'Wow!' I screamed. 'That's it, boy.'

'You like the idea?' he asked.

'Like it? It's wicked. How do we do it?' I was all excited.

It was August 1941 and our dreary style of living and surviving hadn't really changed in any way. We were still dependent on our parents and on the school. Whatever we thought we could do was going to be an uphill attempt all the way. But we seemed ready for whatever might come our way.

Joining the Field Brigade

We had no money so we walked five miles to the Third Field Brigade on Gordon Road, in Rangoon. It turned out to be an outcome not very different from the Charge of the Light Brigade. Even if this looked more like the Charge of the Stupid Brigade, it gave promise of something better. Charlie looked more hopeful than me but I trudged along in the hope that something might just work out.

We got to Major Wade's office and stood outside for a moment, almost uncertain of what could happen. Charlie said, 'You go in first. You're the brave guy.'

I knocked on the door and I heard the Major inside say, 'Come in.'

He gave one look at me and sussed out the 'boy' in me. He quite accurately assessed me as someone who hadn't crossed sixteen. 'How old are you?' he asked.

I hesitated for a moment but then thought I'd go with the truth. 'Sixteen, Sir,' I replied.

'Sonny,' he replied, 'you're just a kid. If you had said eighteen, I could have signed you up.'

My hopes crashed like a bag of potatoes dumped off a loaded buffalo-cart.

There wasn't time to compare notes really, as Charlie knocked and walked in as soon as I'd come out. He may just have noticed my sunken face but was eager to go in and try his luck, though somewhere down he felt he might get a refusal.

'How old are you, lad?' the Major asked.

'Eighteen, Sir,' replied Charlie.

'Come up, here,' said the Major, 'and sign up'.

When I saw Charlie's beaming face I was angry that I had got left out. Then all the 'street learning' I had acquired: the catapult, the forest adventures, the poke-sweet joke and a load of other situations came flashing back through my mind. I was confused and upset but I was determined. I knew I had lost a battle but I was not going to lose the war, even before I could go into any war. I waited for a few more recruits to go in and then quickly slipped in once more. This time I felt sure I could pull it off though the odds looked stacked heavily against me. Somehow I had the funny feeling that the Major wouldn't remember seeing me. I just changed my voice a little to a slightly deeper tone and borrowed a scarf, and tried to look a bit older.

I entered as smartly as I could and heard the familiar question, 'How old are you?'

'I'm eighteen, Sir,' I replied.

'You don't look eighteen,' he said, 'but we'll take you on. Sign up there.'

My heart skipped a beat. I was thrilled. I'd got in. I can't believe my stunt had worked. We both got in: buddies in (home) battles to become buddies in war!

Yet I didn't know what was coming or what to expect. All I seemed to realize was that I was thrown in at the deep end, not only as far as learning and education were concerned but also where this new experience confronted me. This adventure appeared to present itself like an art collection, filled with colourful and colourless pages, but with a blank unpainted front cover. This event perhaps turned out to be the story of my adult life. Yet this new challenge literally just came rolling over us. It hit us with excitement but with frightening uncertainties as well.

Yet, how did the army recruiting fit into the broader picture of war? How were our lives affected? Perhaps this needs a bit of explanation. We were in Burma which was part of the British Empire, even if in some ways, at least in the eyes of the British, Burma was the lesser of the two important parts of their 'India-Burma' Empire. So, as Britain got drawn into the War, Burma too got affected, and so were our lives. Before we could realize it we got totally involved and deeply entrenched.

It was a highly complex situation that Burma found itself in during the 1940s, when life was really just beginning for me. In Europe Britain had to take sides: to raise its profile and its arsenal to assist in curbing the ambitions of a rising Germany under Hitler. In some quarters the situation was more like a keg of gunpowder. The Axis Powers (Germany, Italy and Japan) were winning battles on some fronts. While Germany especially was over-running countries in Europe and Italy was invading countries in the north of Africa, Japan was showing its might in Asia.

The Japanese were now closing in on Indo-China (parts of China, Thailand and Laos) and were already in Burma, with intentions of moving into India. This really meant that they were bound to encounter the British directly at some point. Britain was working desperately to unite the 'forces' (countries working towards freedom) in Europe and was actively trying to get the USA, with its mighty power, involved with the forces in opposing Hitler's conquering army in Europe –the main battle-ground.

Living through the War in Burma: Boyhood Trials Shape The Chindit

Living in Burma during the War

Burma was colonized by Britain following three Anglo-Burmese Wars (1824–1885). British rule brought social, economic, cultural and administrative changes in Burma. The battle for Mandalay was one of the decisive battles fought, and with its fall, all of Burma came under British rule, annexed on 1 January 1886. Later, throughout the colonial era, many Indians arrived as soldiers, civil servants, construction workers and traders. Along with the Anglo-Burmese community, the Indians (not necessarily Anglo-Indians) dominated the commercial and civil life in Burma. Meanwhile Rangoon became the capital of British Burma and an important port between Calcutta and Singapore –two strategic points for the British.

Burmese resentment was strong and was vented in violent riots that paralysed Rangoon constantly from the 1920s until the 1930s. Some of the discontent was caused by the British disrespect for Burmese culture and their ignorance of Burmese traditions, such as the refusal to remove shoes when they entered pagodas°. The British perhaps were not aware that the Buddhist monks were also actively involved in the independence movement. U Wisara, an activist monk, died in prison after a 166-day hunger-strike to protest a rule (seemingly insignificant to the British) that forbade him from wearing his Buddhist robes while imprisoned.

By 1937, Burma became a separately administered colony of Great Britain and Ba Maw became the first Prime Minister of Burma. Ba Maw opposed the participation of Great Britain, and by extension Burma, in World War II. Meanwhile, in 1940, before Japan formally entered the Second World War, Aung

San°, a leading General in Burma at the time, saw no future for Burma if it stayed with Britain. So he moved to Japan to form the Burma Independence Army. This alarmed the British as they counted on the support of Burma together with India. They didn't want Burma slipping away to the Axis Powers who were fighting the united strength of the Allies Forces, where Britain was a major player and an integral part.

The British decided they had to do something about it. They took their cue from the conquering Roman armies who established their prodigious armies by recruiting soldiers and loyal-supporters locally from the people they had conquered. The British had systematically done much of this in India earlier by recruiting, for example, the great 'Babu' army of clerical workers in Bengal. They now did the same in Burma. It is in this massive drive for reinforcements that the two of us 'Charlies' (Charlie Walmsley and I) became 'local' recruits in the British Army.

All this history and involvement didn't really bother us –the Charles-buddies, two headstrong, frustrated teenagers-- building what probably were 'sand-castles' of no value. Yet it was our intent to change our lifestyle. We were ready to grab any opportunity to work out our own independent way of life, even if it meant risk and adventure. Though the army was bound to shackle us in many ways, we felt we had achieved our life-plan towards a life of freedom that we, and no one else, could take responsibility for.

I never consulted my Mum on the matter; afraid that she would have refused me permission. She was very disappointed when she finally got to know about our moves. But I needed to get away from home. Yes, of course I loved Mum, and perhaps my siblings too, and perhaps Dad as well, but as time went by I had lost any love that I may have had for that place --home. Our home environment was volatile quite frequently. There were lots of little things that happened at home that are not really worth remembering or recording. We were never taught to forgive and forget, especially when we were growing up. So we just sat back and harboured ill feelings while getting the benefits of family. There was food on the table and a bed for the night. Nothing else seemed to be part of any agenda. Little vindictive incidents were never analysed or corrected. Unfortunately, as we got older, there wasn't anything or anyone that could change the situation. There was never really any show of affection that might have compensated for unpleasant incidents or behaviour. I cannot remember hugging or cuddling any one in my family.

Army recruiting had purpose

In 1937, when Burma was granted separation from India, British-India was still responsible for Burma's defence in case of war. The new Governor of Burma, Sir Reginald Dorman-Smith, did not totally believe that the Burmans, the majority population (who were the hard-core, first settlers in Burma, who also dominated public thinking) would be loyal to the British. He had some hopes however that the Burmese might just come to their senses and rise up against the Japanese should they attack Burma. But it was General Archibald Wavell, the British commander-in-chief of the army, who realistically assessed that Burma's defence and intelligence lacked strength, training and equipment. It was he who recommended an immediate increase of Battalions.

Trophy D'Souza

That is why in their drive to enrol new recruits they didn't notice that I had gone in a second time (first as an 16-year old, and then as a 18-year old) in the space of an hour. They didn't want any unnecessary checking and cross-checking of lists as it could cause delays in their build-up of the army. Did the Major think I was another boy? Or did he turn a blind eye to my case in his desperation to recruit more soldiers? It was not important. I had got my wish to start a new life. That was all I cared for at that moment.

In 1939 the Burmese army had only approximately four hundred Burmese and three thousand Karens, Kachins° and Chins°, who formed the four Battalions of the Burma Rifles, stationed mainly at Maymyo and Rangoon. There were at the time a few regiments of British troops: Royal Fusiliers, King's own Yorkshire Light Infantry, Gloucester Regiment and the RAMC°. The army was desperate for men. At the time the population of Burma was just 17 million compared to India's 320 million.

By 1941 there was a part-time volunteer Burma Auxiliary Force of four Battalions and a field artillery Battery with First World War vintage *18-Pounders°* --made up of British, Indian, Anglo-Burmese and Anglo-Indians. So, it was clear that in spite of all the recruiting done, Burma might still have had to rely heavily on India in the event of an attack.

Chapter 9

Training Schedules and adventure

The army training began with two weekly parades and basic army tactics for the recruits --order arms, present arms, clean your rifle, pull through, cut off and so on. From then on the rifle was to be our life-saver. We were taught how to look after it and handle it properly. We were then taken to the shooting range, where we shot at different objects. Here my expertise in the use of the catapult, as a young boy, came in handy. I enjoyed this exercise as it came naturally to me. Somehow I began to like this new-found job in quite an adventurous and yet instructive way. It was much better than school and definitely more enjoyable than all academic learning. But the training in 1941 was not really very intense. There was no time for actual training. It was just the basics we were getting into.

It was perhaps a way of getting us initiated into the army. I for one began to understand, for the first time (after all the excitement of recruitment and initial training), what the army really was about and how it was actually organized. It is quite a complex organization to the average outsider. The Army° is divided into Divisions: each Division° is made up of 3 Brigades; each Brigade° had 3 Battalions; each Battalion° had

Trophy D'Souza

3 Companies; each Company° had 3 Platoons; each Platoon° had 3 Sections; each Section° had 8 Soldiers. A Battery° had 8 Field Guns. Each Field Gun° had to be manned by at least 4 soldiers.

One day at our usual parade we were told that we were conscripted immediately. That meant we were now enrolled and liable to serve in the armed forces, as directed by our King and Country (i.e. England, which basically meant the British command in Burma). It also meant we could not go home. The army Barracks were to be our new accommodation. We were given our kits –ill-fitting bucket shorts that came down to our knees and a kit bag with not much in it. The larger sizes of uniforms were designed for British soldiers who perhaps were slightly bigger-built. By comparison we were smaller and slimmer, and looked baggy and clumsy somewhat like ill-fitting fatigues.

The main strategic planners and the administrators in Burma thought an attack could come from the north. They weren't really sure of what to expect. They were certainly surprised when Singapore fell to the Japanese. All that the Brits knew was that an attack on Burma was imminent, and that Burma was not at all ready for a defensive operation. The Royal Air Force was not well-equipped with fighters and bombers. Basically Burma was faced with an enemy who was well-trained and well-equipped, far out-numbering the combined strength of the British, Burmese and Indian troops who were available.

With Singapore in the hands of the enemy, the Japanese air force flew without opposition throughout Malaysia, via the gateways of Siam (now Thailand) and along the Tenasserim°

coastal region to the south east of Myanmar. Moulmein° was caught unawares when it experienced its first air raid on the 23rd December 1941. The people in Rangoon panicked. Many left the city to escape to the North.

One day in the Platoon I heard shouts of, 'Where is Stephenson?'

'Who is Stephenson?' was the repeated enquiry from one of my Officers.

'It's me,' I replied to the group Officer in the Section of the Platoon.

'Your mother's outside,' one of my mates told me. I was happy to see Mum.

She said, 'Son, we're leaving the house. The Japs are coming. Rangoon is not safe anymore. I am going to Maymyo to stay with Aunt Enid. You take care.'

Mum's sister, Enid Vaughan, and her family were there. Mum left, leaving behind all the household goods. She only took along a bundle of clothes.

Chapter 10
Getting deeper into war mode

Meanwhile it was all happening. The first bombing of Rangoon by the Japanese Air Force was on Christmas day, 1941. I had a great time trying to shoot the enemy with my *.303 rifle* while I was on guard duty at the wharves. It was great to be sixteen: I felt invincible. I was sure I could wipe out the enemy. I felt no fear at all.

The Japanese were advancing very fast. Their air force was targeting Rangoon's Mingaladon Airport and the city itself. The British force was not strong in numbers to hold Rangoon. The Japanese outnumbered them by eight to one. As Rangoon could no longer be defended, it was inevitable that all army personnel and civilians had to be evacuated.

I was with the Fifth Battery, training on the guns, the old *18 Pounders* with big wheels, used during the First World War, which were very heavy and difficult to manoeuvre. We were given orders to blow up the guns. After we'd done that, we jumped onto the trucks taking us to Yenangyaung°, the oil refinery on the River Irrawaddy in central Burma. We stayed at the vacant high school there for a month.

Trophy D'Souza

Overstaying Army leave

By the 24th February, 1942, Rangoon's hustle and bustle had gone. It had become dreary: a 'city of silence' with no people around. It was left to a few Air Force planes to continue the attack on the advancing enemy. As the British-led army retreated, we were given orders to pull out and march on to the north, to Mandalay, Burma's old capital, built by the great King Mindon°, a monarch revered by both his people and by the British occupiers. His rule from 1853 to 1878 brought significant changes and stability to Burma until the British interfered with their annexation, first of lower Burma and then later of the rest of Burma during the rule of his brother, Pagan. Mindon's son, Thibaw, was deported to India after Burma was annexed.

Along the way we had to maintain the regime of parades and drills, and kept marching to keep fit. When we arrived in Mandalay, in central Burma, the officers said, 'If anybody has family in Mandalay or Maymyo° you can have ten days' leave.'

Maymyo was 42 miles, further north, from Mandalay. Half way along the journey, at the twenty-first mile stop-point, the whole of Mandalay city could be seen including River Irrawaddy, which I think is one of the most beautiful rivers in the world. I then travelled along the hairpin bends to climb to the plateau. Maymyo has always been described as beautiful and picturesque. It was a town best described as being more European than Burmese though a fairly large Anglo-Burmese population lived there. After the hot and sticky feel of lower Burma Maymyo's cool climate, with its beautiful gardens, brilliant blue skies and pine-tree aromas was indeed a refreshing change. I was thrilled to see my family again and mightily relieved to be away from the theatre of war in Rangoon.

While I was there Dad suffered another stroke and was rushed to the Burma Military Hospital (BMH). He was admitted there because I was in the army. I was now recognized as a British Other Rank (BOR)

At sixteen you tend to forget that army orders must be rigorously followed, with severe penalties for those who disobey them. I overstayed my holiday by one day. On the eleventh day when I reached Mandalay I was shocked to find that the Fifth Battery had left. I was in real panic. Where had they gone? When did they leave? What was I to do? I'd never experienced panic like this in all the years of growing up in the army.

I just could not understand why they had left without me. Did they doubt my loyalty? Did they doubt my commitment to army life? All I knew was that I felt deserted. I then figured out that the best decision was to go back to Maymyo. At my Aunt's place, where all my family were, it was such a relief to talk to Mum about all my troubles and adventures.

Meanwhile news had arrived on the 7th March, 1942, that Rangoon had to be evacuated by the British. Two days later, on the 9th March, Rangoon had been taken by the Japanese. Mum had received a letter telling her that all army personnel families would be evacuated. They had to report to St Michael's School, in Rangoon, on the 11th March, which happened to be my Mum's birthday.

My Aunt told the family who had assembled there, 'No, we are not going.'

My Mum replied, 'All right, but I am going. Maymyo is not safe from the Japanese.'

Trophy D'Souza

So she wrapped a few bundles and went to the hospital to see Dad and the doctors.

The doctors advised her, 'Mrs Stephenson, if we get the chance we will send him across. But you have to go because you will not get another chance.'

She packed a few essentials of clothing for the girls and boys, as much as she was allowed to take. They left for Myitkyina° air-strip in the northern tip of Burma, a point that was close to China as well. From there planes would take them to safety in India. At Myitkyina the Stephensons from Moulmein --my Dad's brother, his wife and their six children-- were all there. Mum was so happy to see her in-laws and was relieved to know that she was not alone. She had Dad's family there which was of great comfort to her. The two families were happy to stay together waiting for a plane to rescue them though they didn't have a clue about when the aircraft would arrive.

The aircrafts used to evacuate the people were mostly flown by Pan-American Airways pilots, in response to an appeal from the Tenth Air Force. In the final count around 14000 people were flown out by the American airmen. People were charged Rupees 280 per person, which in today's money would be about 20 cents.

Coping with loss in Maymyo

I was able to stay back in Maymyo. I visited Dad every day. One day, when Dad was not looking his best (actually looking helpless with tubes all over), he turned to me and signalled with his hands that he was dying. At first I thought that he was only a little depressed. When I did realize what he was saying, I cried my heart out. I then tried to reassure him, 'Dad, I will be back.'

We were not paid during the retreat so I had no money on me. I ran all the way to my Aunt's place to tell them about Dad. My Uncle offered his support, 'Don't worry, Charles. I will come with you and see what can be done.'

When we got to the hospital, Dad was not there. His bed had been removed. What had happened to Dad? Had they buried him in a hurry with no sign to mark at the spot? The mystery remains, and to this day I do not know what really happened to my Dad. The hospital suddenly seemed empty. In a short space of time all the nurses had left. Only the chief Surgeon and a few Orderlies were still there.

I approached the Major in charge at Maymyo, 'Excuse me, Sir. I am from the Fifth Field Battery: they have all left and the last I have heard is that they left through the Kabaw° valley going towards Imphal° in northern India. I've got no one to attach myself to. Could I join your little group?'

There were only nine of them in the group, including the Major. He agreed, 'OK! Come along.' We jumped into the waiting truck and left for Mandalay.

Chapter 11
Evacuating positions and retreat

The evacuation of the sick and wounded to India was first done from Shewbo° airport. During the last week of April Shewbo was heavily bombed, which meant that Myitkyina air-strip in the north was the only exit left for evacuation by air.

From Mandalay we took a train to Myitkyina. Along the way there was a derailment ahead, which meant our train slowed down to a crawl. The lines were blocked but the railway officials got their teams working round the clock to clear the lines to keep traffic moving. We were two days on that journey when the lines finally got completely blocked.

Apparently in his desperation to get away from the Japanese advance a Chinese army official had stolen a train at gunpoint to try and escape to Myitkyina, He crashed it 25 miles on, blocking the line for two days. The Chinese° (then Nationalist China) too had offered to support the British and Allied Forces in the War. Their earlier support to the Axis Powers switched to the Allied Forces after Japan bombed the Allied Forces at Pearl Harbour in 1941.

The Major called us together and discussed the situation with us. 'We're in a bit of a tight situation. We've not even reached Mogaung°. We've really only come as far as Samaw°. We've no choice but to start walking from here. Also, there's only one route and it's through the Hukaung° valley.'

This valley was meshed with a vast overgrown forest and numerous rivulets draining into the River Chindwin°. During the monsoons a great part of the Hukaung was flooded making it dangerous and impossible to cross. The valley was also infested with tigers and other wild animals. After the war the valley was referred to as Death Valley as many refugees and retreating army personnel died from disease while trekking to India.

Backpacking across Rivers

Slinging our packs on to our backs, we started the walk. I was young, fit and strong, and could walk for miles. It wasn't really much of a problem for me, thanks to all the walking I'd done along the train lines from school, saving my train-fare for a better lunch. That really proved to be a sturdy training for war or perhaps a blessing in disguise. I do not know how many miles we walked before we came to River Chindwin. This was a tributary of River Irrawaddy, used frequently by traders as it is navigable by shallow-draught steamers. We managed to cross it using bamboo rafts and poles. Fortunately after this the terrain turned flatter, which was welcome relief to us all as it made walking a lot more pleasant. I think by now we had covered about 160 kms.

At the foot of the hills we stopped at a village. We soon found out that we were not the only ones retreating. There were other soldiers who had separated from their Commands. We managed to get some rest in a spare hut provided by the villagers. That day it rained in torrents. In the hut my new-found friends were boiling water in a four-gallon tin. They did this by placing the tin full of water on two green bamboo poles placed over some bricks, with the fire underneath. A bunch of tea leaves was thrown into the tin with boiling water and soon the aroma of fresh tea filled the air. This was going to be the best cuppa in months --for a bunch of ragged-looking, back-trekking, semi-rudderless, quasi-disheartened, desperately thirsty fighters!

We took off our boots and socks to air our tired feet. After some time the bamboo poles holding the tin of water burnt through. Soon the inevitable had to happen: the tin collapsed. The boiling water rushed onto my feet. Quite strangely I was the only one that was scalded quite badly by the hot water. Huge blisters developed in a few minutes. My insteps were like two great balloons. All I remember was that I was in excruciating pain.

There was nothing really that the Major could do for me. There were some Sikh soldiers in the group of us who had taken shelter in the village but they would not take orders from anyone. The Major approached one of them and asked, 'Would you please take this man on one of your horses? Could you let him do it for a few days, while you walk alongside?'

'No,' was his prompt reply.

The riders and their horses left. I cannot condemn them for not wanting to help. Any delay would have meant falling into the enemy's hands. No one was sure what to expect but every British soldier knew that the Japanese would show no mercy to anyone who fell into their hands. It was a case of 'each-to-his-own.' Good Samaritans° in those days were few and far between.

The group I was with did not wish to delay their journey. They too left without me. I never saw them again. For everyone it was not only a race to escape the enemy but also a race to avoid the dreaded monsoon. Once the rains started a great area of the valley would be flooded making it impossible to get across.

I trudged along with my feet aching unbearably. The large blisters rubbed against stones and sticks and leaves. With sheer determination I managed to climb up the mountain and then down the mountain again. Never in my life have I walked in mud without my shoes. But now even with my blisters I had no choice. Eventually the blisters burst. To my surprise I found that the mud had healing properties. In fact within three days the pain had gone. What a relief and what a blessing! The skin had dried with the mud: a sort of first-aid service provided by nature. I was keen to tell my nurse and doctor friends how this worked miraculously for me. Meanwhile I just kept walking bare-foot in the slush until I could wear my boots again.

Lending a hand to Captain

As I trekked up the next mountain I met a Captain sitting under a tree. He was a podgy little fellow. 'Would you please give me a hand?' he begged.

I felt sorry for him. 'OK,' I said.

He asked, 'Walk with me, please.'

He could barely walk and this was holding me up. I stayed with him for three days. Every night as we slept in the jungle, just the two of us, we could hear tigers, jackals, hyenas, monkeys and the buzz of mosquitoes. It was really crazy and scary. The noise of the jungle at night was more than frightening at times.

One night while we were sleeping on this little track that had been made by people walking ahead of us, we could hear an animal approaching us.

I asked the Captain, 'How can we start a fire?'

The Captain pulled out a large looking pill and said to me, 'I have a couple of matches.'

I lit the pill and it burned for a considerable amount of time, I managed to collect some dry leaves and sticks and made a nice little fire. It kept us warm and also kept the wild animals at bay.

Unfortunately the Captain could only manage four or five miles a day. I knew that if I stayed with him I would never get to India and might even die of starvation. After much serious thought I had to come to a serious but painful decision. On the third day, early in the morning before he could wake up, I slipped away.

I felt very guilty about leaving the poor Captain to his fate. But I felt that if I wanted to survive I would have to just keep going on as fast as my legs could carry me. I think I said some prayers: I prayed for my own safety and asked God to protect the Captain too. I don't think I was ever able to find out what happened to the Captain. I kept walking: uphill first, and then downhill; uphill, downhill –it seemed to go on forever. Eventually all I could think of was my own survival. I could not see any trekkers ahead of me, or behind me. I was completely alone. I did not have a clue about how far ahead my companions were. I also had to face another frightening truth: there was no way I could find any food to eat.

Chapter 12

Walking fears and Death Valley

Then, finally, I reached the most dreaded part of the journey, Death Valley. All along the way there were dead people --some sitting up against the tree, others holding jewellery or piles of money. Most of these skeletons of people happened to be Indians, who apparently could not carry or protect their life-savings. There was no way I could even be tempted to take any of it though there was so much of it for the taking. I did not have the energy to carry the belongings I had with me leave alone take anything more. As the days went by my body began to tire mainly because I hadn't eaten for days.

Apparently disease --cholera, dysentery, malaria, and exhaustion --seem to have been the main causes of the deaths along the trail. Thousands died on this trek. It was indeed a pitiful sight. I knew I had no time for pity and sorrow. I just had to move on. Fortunately I was young and my earlier trials in life had not only toughened my body but had also strengthened my resolve to survive. I kept going even though every bone in my body ached. At one stage I was very near exhaustion. I wondered if I too would meet my end here in Death Valley.

Trophy D'Souza

Finally I reached a village in Nagaland (north-eastern India). People feared these villagers but I found them very kind. They gave me a place to rest and something to eat. The next day when I left I was given some raw rice which I carried in my pockets. I munched raw rice along the way. After twenty-one days of trekking I finally reached a mountain. I was exhausted but with sheer determination I walked on alone. I came to a small waterfall with a bamboo grove nearby. I stopped to drink some water and noticed that the track was getting wider. This gave me hope.

Perhaps, I began to believe, this was it: India! Perhaps it would be behind this mountain. But when I reached the top of the mountain, I did not see any signs of human living. I looked across only to see mountains on top of mountains, spreading as far as the eye could see --like a great sea of green, which seemed to go on forever, fading away into the grey horizon. Perhaps it was the first of the Assam Ranges. I was reminded of the nursery song, 'The bear went over the mountain...'

Finding peace in Creation

I spoke aloud in dismay, 'How am I to get through all this? Where am I? What am I to do?'

All hope of reaching India faded. I felt I could not go on. I was weary and depressed, I could think only of rest. I walked back to the little waterfall flowing gently down a stream, took off my boots and put my tired feet into the water. The cool water relieved my aching feet as I sat there puffing and panting. Then I looked at the view in front of me: it was one of the most beautiful sights I had ever seen. All of a sudden I felt closure –with God and his creation-- and a feeling of calm descended on me. The quietness of the mountain was relaxing so I took the opportunity to enjoy a much-needed rest, almost totally oblivious of anything happening around me.

As I sat idly by this waterfall the whole day I did not see a single person pass by. Every now and then negative thoughts clouded my mind. I wanted to give up and just stay there and die. But as day light was slowly fading I kept saying to myself, 'I cannot stay in this place alone.' So I prayed, 'Help me, O Lord my God.' I also prayed to Virgin Mary, His mother. The prayers I had learnt somewhere in school came back to me, 'Our Father' and 'Hail Mary'. I felt strength come back to me, to my legs!

I had wasted a whole day relaxing and cooling my feet. I began to feel anxious. So I composed myself and got my mind to think positively. I encouraged myself to continue regardless, 'I've got to catch up to somebody.'

I put on my boots, got up and started down the mountain. I still cannot believe my luck. As I walked past the bend, right there in the valley, right below, was a little puffer engine doing a little shunting. Oh! What a beautiful sight: a train puffing along the line. It was about two or three thousand feet down and I knew that soon I would be in town, in some human company.

I was so excited that I had made it that instead of going along the path-way I went straight down, just charging down wildly. I felt the mad rush of blood and all I kept saying to myself was, 'Keep going! Keep going!'

Then I felt my leg step onto something soft. My leg caved in. 'What's this?' I mused.

Trophy D'Souza

I looked down and saw a horrible sight. My leg was inside the chest of some unfortunate person. I was too excited to reach the engine below to worry about the poor dead soul. I pulled my leg out, rolled over and fell, and then rolled again. I kept rolling down the mountain --rolling, rolling down relentlessly (almost like the way the water comes down at Lodore°).

I kept getting up, catching hold of branches, rolling again, falling down, pulling myself up here and pulling myself up there. It seemed like the rush of the excitement had provided fuel enough to run another hundred miles. In fact I hardly needed energy or a sense of direction. I knew where I was heading and I knew I could just roll! I couldn't stop to think. My brain had reached 'release gear'. Then, before I could realise it, I was down there!

Seeing Land –a sight of joy

I ran and ran along the track as fast as my legs could carry me until I reached the puffing train. I knew a bit of Hindi° because I had learnt to chat with my 'untouchable'° friends back in Rangoon. I asked the driver, 'Where is the camp?'

He pointed along the railway track and said, 'Three miles.'

I walked along the tracks and came across the camp – Tinsukia (in upper Assam). Never did a sight of tents look so beautiful. Perhaps it was a sight more satisfying than the one Wordsworth° saw on London Bridge. It was truly 'more fair' and more 'touching' because even though it wasn't really morning when I got there the relief I felt was incredible. At last I was not alone. Soon the friendly people there offered me all the help I craved for. Somehow at that point I wasn't hungry. I just wanted to lie down and sleep...for a hundred years!

In the mean time back in Burma, Maymyo had been bombed. It had to be the target as it was the Army Headquarters. On Good Friday, 6th April, 1941 Mandalay was shelled, and the hospital and the railway station were destroyed. On 4th May the Governor, Dorman-Smith, under direct orders from Churchill, in the UK, flew out of Burma from Myitkyina airport. On 6th May the airport was bombed. The 2300 wounded men, who had not yet been evacuated, had no option but to walk to India with many other civilians and army personnel. Those who took the route through the Kabaw Valley into Imphal were more fortunate compared to those who trekked through the Hukaung Valley.

By 28th May practically all the troops had crossed the border into India. Some 13 000 men were killed, wounded, or missing, besides those who had been evacuated as sick. The Japanese losses apparently were 4600 killed and wounded.

Chapter 13

Relaxing in friendly territory

The next week we were transferred first to Margarita in north Assam, for a short while, and then on to Howrah, in Bengal, a town joined to Calcutta across the River Hooghly (a tributary of the River Ganges) by the famous Howrah Bridge, a cantilever bridge, the sixth longest of its type in the world.

At the Howrah train station I was asked by a British Army Officer, 'Are you a BOR?'

'Yes, Sir,' I replied, 'very proud to be a soldier of His Majesty's Forces.'

'Get in,' he said. I jumped into the truck, happy to be with my fellow BOR's. We were driven to the Calcutta Racecourse barracks. This was to be our temporary station until they sorted out our details and regiments. Our sleeping quarters were not very comfortable. They were actually the stands of the racecourse. No one complained probably because we were just lucky to have survived the retreat. As I lay resting on the not-so-comfortable stand my thoughts once again ran riot.

'Oh my God,' I exclaimed to myself. 'Have I done the right thing in coming out to India? Have my family come across or are they still in Burma?'

Trophy D'Souza

I was quite confused. Yes, I was really worried. When my turn came to see the Board and the RTO, a very nice guy, a Captain by rank, he asked me, 'Lad, would you like to have a holiday and go somewhere?'

I replied, 'Sir, where to?' Yes, indeed: Where to?

'I don't know,' he said. 'But when you do decide, let me know.' He continued, 'We don't know where the Fifth Field Battery is but we are trying to make enquiries. As soon as we find out you will find it on the notice board.'

I returned to my temporary sleeping quarters, the racecourse stand, and had a couple of nights of reasonably restful sleep there, waiting patiently for the next order to arrive, just praying that all would be well for me.

One day as fate would have it, an army officer who was passing by stopped at my bench. He singled me out and asked, 'Aren't you Stephenson?'

'Yes,' I answered, quite surprised as I didn't know what to expect.

'Your parents are up in Lahore,' he continued. 'I'll come back and speak to you again.'

I could not believe my luck. He never came back but in those hurried comments he did say that they were staying near the Punjab Club.

In my excitement I rushed to the RTO and asked, 'Excuse me, Sir, could I have my Warrant°?'

'Yes,' he replied quite cheerily. 'Where do you want to go?'

'Lahore°, Sir,' I promptly replied.

He wrote out a Warrant and handed it to me saying, 'Here you are: Second Class BOR Warrant to Lahore.'

I was driven to Howrah railway station with many other soldiers going on furlough°. I did not know where Lahore was --my geography was not very good. At the train station I made enquiries about the train that would take me to my destination. I was given instructions to catch the Punjab-Mail.

As there was time to spare before the departure of the train I decided to get something to eat. The RTO had given me Rupees 20 (about $10 in today's money). I bought a little snack from one of the platform food kiosks.

Then I waited eagerly for the train to come into the platform of this terminus station. This was my first experience of the Indian trains. I'd never imagined what I saw unfold, all the excitement that surrounds the almost uncontrolled rush of people moving towards the platforms and the trains. India was not like Burma. It was crowded with people rushing around everywhere, on the streets and even here on the platforms of this station. I was not aware of how quickly they moved and literally scramble for what they want or are looking for. When rushing for seats on the train they were too quick for me. I had to push my way through in order just to get a seat on the train. When I finally managed to squeeze into a compartment I looked with dismay to find that there were no seats available in the Second Class compartments. Of course with so many people who had saved their pennies there couldn't possibly be a place in the Third Class compartments.

Never have I seen so many people on a train. Catching a train in India has to be experienced to be believed. Where did all these people come from? People were sitting on top of the roofs of the carriages, hanging out of the train doors, hanging on to whatever was available just to get on to the train. If they

Trophy D'Souza

could have they would have sat underneath the train. I had to use all my muscle power to push my way through. Politeness would have got me nowhere.

But I thought I'd give it a shot. I approached the ticket collector, 'I have a Second-Class Warrant, Sir.'

He replied, 'I am sorry. The Brits probably won't let you in --the English, I mean. They jam themselves into the Second Class. And if you are coloured, that is it, mate.'

Well, I never got in. Hope was in sight when he said, 'You give me five rupees (about $3 in today's money) and I'll fix something.'

I gave him the five rupees and he took me to the servants' compartments. I got in as I had no choice. But before I could decide which seat to sit in, as the compartment was empty, the carriage was filled with Sikhs, pushing and shoving. They occupied all the seats and I was forced to sit on the floor.

It was a long, long journey. It took three days and two nights to get to Lahore. And where do you think I slept? There were these long hat racks almost touching the ceiling of the carriage. Yes, believe it or not, I got up there and managed to get a good night's rest.

It would have been of no use explaining to the Sikhs about the hardships I had endured. They would certainly not have understood because I looked too young to be believed. I just took what I got and did not complain. The most important thing on my mind was to see my family. As I lay there in the discomfort of the rack, I began to feel very excited about getting to Lahore and about being reunited with my family once again. I was overcome with emotion as tears began rolling down. I soon fell asleep and just let nature do its work.

Chapter 14
Travelling hassles --ordinary style

Lahore has over a thousand years of history. It was the capital of the Sikh Empire before the British took over, and under British rule it was the capital of the entire state of Punjab. Renowned for its cultural and educational centres, it has been described by writers as a romantic place, which inspired many famous writers to write poetry and literature. The most famous of these was Rudyard Kipling. There is in fact a saying, 'He who has not been to Lahore is yet to be born.' Described as a city of gardens, Lahore is also a festive city. It is the second most densely populated city in Pakistan very close to the border of India, in the north. At the time it was part of British-India. The train ride from Howrah station to Lahore was a journey across the entire expanse of northern India --from east to west.

After the long journey to Lahore we finally arrived at the city's station. I reported to the RTO there and enquired, 'Excuse me, Sir! Could you tell me where the evacuee camp is?'

'Sorry, but I do not know of any evacuee camp here,' he replied.

This puzzled me but I thanked him all the same. I then stepped outside and hailed a tonga (a small carriage drawn by a horse), colourfully decorated with all kinds of tassels. 'Punjab Club,' I said to the tonga man.

The driver took me there. On the outside it looked like a very posh place, but opposite the club was an old house, dilapidated with neglect. At the front of the club was a huge arch. The window panes on the main building were all broken, and creepers and little plants had found their way in through the brick work. 'No one would live here,' I thought to myself. The place was silent and appeared haunted. I was reminded of De La Mare's° poem, '*The Listeners*'. 'Is there anybody there?' I asked myself very much the way the Traveller in the poem asks. I soon felt certain that no one could possibly be living there.

'This can't be the place,' I said to myself rather loudly, in Hindi.

The tonga driver impatiently replied, 'We'll go one more round.'

The tonga driver was losing his patience. He wanted to drop me off somewhere. I asserted my authority as he turned around to return and said, 'No, no, no you go back to the Punjab Club.'

A policeman nearby noticed us arguing and wanted to know what was going on. After hearing my story he ordered the driver to take me where I wanted to go. We decided to try this old house again. I walked towards the huge arch way again but this time I ventured in. I could hear voices in the distance. Behind this arch there was another house and my gut feeling told me that I had reached my destination.

I called the tonga man in. He was pleased to witness the reunion of mother and son, surrounded by the whole Stephenson gang. I was so happy they were alive and they too naturally were so excited to see me. There was a lot of kissing, hugging and crying, and everyone talking at the same time. It was so good to see one's family again, all safe and sound. It was also such a relief to see bread again. I was so hungry that I ate a whole loaf of bread with just butter. To me that was a banquet. The lost son had returned home.

My furlough came to an end far too quickly as it was time to return to Howrah railway station. When I returned to the racecourse I walked straight to the notice board. I saw that the Fifth Field Battery was in a place called Mhow, in northern India.

I informed the RTO, 'Sir, I've found out now that our Battery is in Mhow.'

He issued me a warrant and once again I saw myself at the crowded Howrah station. But this time I was experienced and had some idea of how I could handle the rush for the train. I pushed and shoved like everyone else and managed to get a seat in the third class compartment. On arrival at Mhow train station, I was pleased to find that an Army Officer was there everyday to assist soldiers who were travelling.

He approached me, 'You're from the Auxiliary Force?'

'Yes, Sir.'

'Come on, jump in,' he indicated with his hand.

I was the only armed force person off the train that day. I jumped into the small 15 cwt truck that took me to the lines --Malcolm Barracks, in Mhow.

We were not very long at the place when we were taken to our tents. After some time an officer paid me a visit saying, 'You've just come out. You had better go on a holiday. Here is your warrant for four weeks.'

Trophy D'Souza

Not really thinking about the involvement I replied truthfully, 'Sir, I've already had two.'

It was too late to retract as the officer gave me a warrant to Lahore for another two weeks. My family were overjoyed and I had another chance to relax in this very festive and beautiful city.

After my leave I returned to my new base. Orders had arrived that the new *25 pounders* were ready and we were to be posted soon. So the Fifth Field Battery --A Troop and B Troop-- moved to Ranchi, a beautiful place in the state of Bihar, which had a climate similar to that of Maymyo.

The city of Ranchi is situated in the valley of Chotanagpur and lies 2140 feet (app 650 metres) above sea level. It is well known for its waterfalls. The climate is cool and temperate, and its numerous temple complexes are the city's attraction. Ranchi is on the South Eastern Railway and is connected directly to Calcutta.

At our base in Ranchi I was placed into the A troop on *Number 4* gun. We trained to perfect our usage of these pounders. There were five soldiers assigned to manage each gun. The positions assigned to the gun were numbered 1, 2, 3, 4, and 5. The team rotated through each number, so that every member of the team was familiar with all four positions 2, 3, 4, and 5. Only the gun sergeant was assigned to Number 1. Those assigned to number four and five positions were given the task of loading the guns. Number three was assigned the task called Laying --that is the precise task of firing the gun. He has to know where to fire and how to fire by adjusting the gun to an elevation between -5° to 45°. And Number 2 and Number 3 had the task of turning the gun along its 360° rotating base.

I could do the loading job, but the laying task was too confusing for me. What was elevation? What were degrees? I could not understand how it all worked. And in those days I did not know that 360° rotation was a circle. How could I possibly be a Layer? So I befriended the best Layer of the group and explained my predicament.

I requested, 'Every time I'm number three, would you please run into number three's place and I'll go to Number 4?' He agreed.

I eventually told the rest of the team and they said, 'OK. You be the Loader.'

We went through the routine many times and each time I was assigned Number 3, I ran to Number 4 and my friend ran to Number 3 for me. That's how I overcame a hurdle that stemmed from my lack of education.

After a few more drills with the guns we were sent to the Firing Range. After a few rounds of firing I was shaking like a leaf, not because of fear, because I had come down with a dreaded malaria attack. The NCO Orderly informed me that my temperature had reached 105°F. He informed the Battery Commander to transfer me to the hospital immediately, but the Officer refused. After a couple of days the fever did not subside and this time I was vomiting. The Commanding Officer was informed and I was taken to the hospital. After admission to the British Military Hospital I was given a blood test. It showed that I had the MT (malignant type) malaria, which can be fatal. With quinine treatment (and a bottle of beer) everyday, I recovered.

Trophy D'Souza

At the hospital the English nurses were very dutiful, checking my temperature every hour. In those days I was probably quite an attractive young man. There was this one nurse who would always give me a kiss on the lips and leave. I was burning with fever and her lips felt cool on my warm lips. It was quite an exciting experience for me --I have never kissed anyone before, never really experienced sexual desires, never masturbated-- the Brothers at boarding school would have punished me if they had found out I had any weaknesses in that area.

I was brought up with a strict discipline both at home and at school. Swearing was not tolerated, and I never once uttered words like 'bloody' or 'damn', for fear that my parents would punish me. I do not remember hearing or using abusive words among my friends. It was not proper and they would not have been tolerated in society. I was always polite and that made me earn the respect of people and as far as I can remember I was liked by most of the men around me. I did my best to hide the fact that I was not well-educated. But in the general run of things this proved to be of no concern. I felt rather pleased that I could at least write my name as there were some who couldn't even do that. They just used a cross in place of their signature to collect their pay packet. This was a confidence boost for me as I found out that were people who were worse off than me.

While I was in hospital recuperating from my malaria attack, the Battery was told that the guns were to be taken away. Our Battalion was to be disbanded and a new Division was being formed under the name of the Burma Intelligence Corps. Everyone was to report to Mhow. When I was discharged from the hospital only a few people were left there cleaning and tiding up the place.

I reported to the Officer in Charge who explained the situation and then gave me an option, 'Do you want to go back to the guns? If you do, you will go into the Coast Battery and you will have to go to Calcutta.'

I replied, 'No sir, I would like to go to the Burma Intelligence Corps.'

'Well,' he replied 'you will go onto Number 8 Platoon.'

'Thank you, Sir.' I saluted, turned around and marched off.

Chapter 15

Training for intelligence and skills

In *Platoon 8* our rigorous training began. The usual guard duty, parades, inspection, drill and rifle practice were all there except that it was more intense compared to the training we had done in 1941. There was one problem: we had to put up with Captain Hunter. He was Anglo-Indian, and he was ambitious, tough and pretentious. One day while I was on guard duty, standing straight and tall, my rifle sparkling clean, my uniform well-pressed and buttoned, looking a perfect sentry, the Captain passed by. I gave him my best salute, proud to be on duty, serving my country, when he stopped and put me on charge --it meant I would be compounded, i.e. I would be given a suspension, a minor punishment.

The Guard Commander asked, 'For what, Sir?'

He barked, 'That is none of your business. Just give him two weeks.' I was given two weeks.

Well, those higher up must have got some feedback on Captain Hunter's performance. All we knew was that he did not get the promotion he sought for. He remained a Captain.

Training in Mhow was challenging. We had to study the military operations involved in Intelligence work, which basically was spying. One day we were told to assemble at the hall. Our Platoon Commander, Captain Barrett --one of the old- fashioned type, a fatherly man and a thorough gentleman-- came in to address us.

He enquired, 'Anyone here who wants to volunteer to go into *Platoon 3*? They are training to go behind the enemy lines. It is very dangerous, I'm warning you. So, if any of you want to see some action, put up your hand.'

I put up my hand. 'You know, I am telling you, Stephenson, it's going to be bad.'

I replied, 'Sir, when they broke us up at Ranchi most of my friends went to *Platoon 1, 2 or 3*. I'll go to *Platoon 3*, Sir.'

Luck was on my side. Someone had backed out from there because he was afraid. I took his place and was transferred to Jhansi in northern India.

The Officers at Jhansi were a remarkable group of Majors and Captains, near prefect gentleman, who had given up their well-paid jobs in big private companies to fight for King and country. I had great respect for them. As soon as I arrived at the base, I met my Platoon Commander, Major Lutenbrain, a proper gentleman.

He gave me my orders: 'You are going to the First Battalion South Staffordshire Regiment. Pack your bags. You'll leave tomorrow.'

If I thought the training at the Fifth Field Battery was tough, this was even more intensive here in the Battalion. Before the retreat the army recruits were given very basic training. They were not ready to face a well-trained Japanese army. The commanding officers all agreed that to retake

Burma we would have to get tougher with our attack drills and endurance manoeuvres.

We were trained to use every weapon that was available --the rifle, Thompson's sub- machine guns, Bren guns, Sten guns-- and we were able to fire them from the hip. Our commanders placed an importance on patrolling, which is the basis of success in jungle warfare. It was arduous training: jungle shooting, column marching, digging, signals and patrols. We were drilled until we learned to move confidently. When a soldier is defeated in war he sees himself as the hunted. It was important to feel that we were hunting a Japanese, not he us. Training became real, disciplined and assertive, but no training, even one so intensive, could prepare us for what was to come.

Training for social bonding

I remember an interesting incident while training in the earlier part of the course. My team mates had gone for a swim. In those days I was really very shy. At school we bathed with our trousers on. We were never allowed to remove all our clothes in public. We always had to have something on. I was surprised to see the British soldiers who had no inhibition about exposing their bodies: they stripped and jumped into the river without any embarrassment. I stood watching with envy from the bank, fully dressed, quite inhibited and extremely shy.

One of my mates shouted, 'Hey Steve! Come on in, come on.'

All I did was to say, 'No, no, no.'

One after the other kept calling out to me, 'Over here, come on, come on.'

Under this mounting pressure I gave it a second thought. I reasoned with myself, 'Well, if I am going to be with these chaps, I had better get in, or else I might become the butt of their jokes.'

So, without another invitation, I slipped off my clothes and plunged in.

My God! It wasn't just yelling and whistling. The Brits nearly belted out their 'Jerusalem' anthem. 'Hurray!' they blasted. 'We're not after your brown eye.' I laughed with relief.

They were indeed very friendly buddies --good mates, full of humour, yet hard-hitting fighters. I learned to love them as brothers and appreciated their friendship. We were after all a 'band of brothers', well-trained and tough. In fact, in a war situation the code of success was to 'stick together through thick and thin' for survival.

Winning --the Chindit way

One of the army commanders, who had left a lasting impression on my life, was General Orde Charles Wingate°. This Brit was an eccentric as well as a man of great knowledge. His overbearing manner won him few friends but his 'Chindits'° had unshakable faith in him as their Commander. Unfortunately he did not live to see the end of the war. While flying from Imphal (in India) to a new assignment, his plane crashed into the mountains, on March 24th 1944.

The Chindits of Wingate were named after the mythical griffin, the Chinthe –the half lion and half eagle guardian of the Burmese Temples. The Chindits included the *77 Brigade* commanded by Brigadier Calvert which had four regiments:

the King's, Lancaster Fusiliers, First South Staffordshire and the famous 3/6 Gurkhas°.

In order to target the enemy effectively the British Army created the 'Special Force'° which became effectively the front line of attack. The Special Force consisted of 17 British Battalions, 5 Gurkha Battalions and 3 West African Battalions. The Battalions were then split into two Columns: Lieutenant Colonel Richards manned *Column 38* and Major Ron Dess was in charge of *Column 80*. I was in it, with the Staffordshire as the Burmese Intelligence Corp man. I was proud to belong to the Special Force. We were all part of a long-range penetration Battalion.

A Column Battalion contained four Platoons: a Commando Platoon which included engineers; a Reconnaissance Platoon (mainly Burma Rifles); a Support Platoon consisting of two medium machine guns, two three-inch mortars; an animal Transport Platoon and Column Headquarters including R.A.F. detachment, medical detachment, intelligence section and signals. Every Column had its own doctors and surgeons.

Blocking the Jap advance
The role of the *77 Brigade* was first to land and create an airbase and then to block the routes that were used by the Japanese for communication and supplies. This would entail blowing up a few bridges and blocking the railway north to Mogaung. The estimated time given to us was two to three months for the Special Force mission in Burma. When this was accomplished the Brigade would return to India, their permanent base.

Trophy D'Souza

Finally, when we were ready for the Mission we were driven to Hailakandi°, one of the two airfields built on the Imphal plain. There a great flock of gliders was awaiting us. They were rather unattractive compared to the graceful Dakotas around the edges of the field. These aircrafts would lift the gliders to the sky with hopes of transporting the *77 Brigade*, led by Brigadier Calvert, to the other side of the enemy line. I was in that Brigade. The pilots were practising take-offs and landings. The training was intense. In spite of one of the gliders crashing and killing seven men we had great faith in the American pilots. We believed we could go anywhere with them.

While we were there Lord Louis Mountbatten paid the troops a visit. Admiral Mountbatten, the new Supreme Commander, was optimistic, youthful and gallant. He spoke with such frankness and sincerity that we were inspired with hope that the war would be won. It is noteworthy that after the war Lord Louis Mountbatten became the First Earl Mountbatten of Burma. Here's an extract I remember from Mountbatten's inspiring speech:

'I have come here to look at you …We are not going to quit fighting when it rains. The Japanese don't expect us to fight on. They will be surprised and caught on the wrong foot. We shall fight in all places. We have the finest hospitalisation and air-evacuation scheme that the Far East has ever seen. The Japs have nothing. They will have to fight nature as well as us… And finally: who stated this story about the Jap Superman? I assure you he is not!…Millions of them are slum-dwellers, with no factory laws, no trade unions, no freedom of speech, nothing except an ignorant fanatical idea that their Emperor is God. Intelligent free men can whip them anytime…'

Motivated by Lord Mountbatten's speech, we were ready for action. The whole place was filled with an atmosphere of excitement. There was suspense as well but it was tempered with hope, eagerness and determination. The enemy was soon to be confronted and this time they would face the Special Force --a real force, tactically well-trained-- a very different army from the one that retreated in 1942.

Chapter 16

Invading with stealth and air power

The battle plan was that on 6th March, 1944, some of the troops would be flown in by gliders while the next day the remaining troops were to be taken in by the Dakotas. Captain Stagg my Intelligence Officer (IO) told me, 'Stephenson, you will have to go with the gliders. The rest of the Column will be going on the next night.'

When I got there one of the glider pilots introduced himself as Jackie Coogan. I did not realize who he was at that stage. He was talking a lot about himself and boasted that he was the husband of Betty Grable. Well, I knew of Betty Grable. She was one of the well-known movie stars in our time. I had seen quite a few of her movies in my early teen years. He could not stop bragging about Betty Grable. This was the same guy we saw on television in the Adams family as Festus.

Landing in Broadway

Just before we were to take off, there was a change of plans. Instead of landing in Piccadilly we were to land in Broadway. These were code names for the four landing points around Indaw°, named by Wingate. Broadway was 35 miles east-north-east of Indaw, selected because it was uninhabited. The flat ground was ideal for building an airstrip in a short period of time. What was perhaps most important was that there was water nearby.

That then was to be the night, an ideal one, as a brilliant full moon lit up the sky. It was indeed a perfect night for landing. We were now in the gliders. I do not remember which glider I was in. I was able to find out later I that around fifty gliders took off that night. At about six o'clock in the evening the Dakotas pulling two gliders at a time took off one after the other at half-minute intervals. My feelings were a cocktail mix of excitement and enthusiasm, tension and anxiety. All the caning and whipping endured during my school years had indeed prepared me to withstand failure and to stand up to the harsh demands of daily army training. I felt I was ready for whatever lay ahead.

We circled slowly across the 7000-feet hills surrounding Imphal. We sat very quietly, with no one even smoking. We bumped and swayed, huddled together with our packs, in this rather rickety wooden glider. My stomach churned inside me. It was time for me to say a silent prayer to Mary, the Blessed Virgin, to protect me and give me strength and courage for what was to come. Some in my glider were nodding off but in spite of the discomfort I was in I tried to stay awake and alert.

Crashing of Gliders

As we flew over the target lines the gliders were released from the plane. There was then an eerie silence, and then a bump. It meant that the gliders we were in had landed. Then the unexpected occurred: some of the gliders came crashing down. In fact there were crashes left, right and centre. The underbellies of these aircrafts were being ripped off. Glider pilots and other people on board were almost running on their feet. The mules that were being transported were also dying from the severe wounds they had sustained on landing, with their bottoms nearly scraped off.

Some of the gliders were somersaulting while others came hurtling down, a few getting smashed against trees. The runway by now had quite a few ditches created. There were log tracks as well, made in the monsoon by logs pulled by elephants. These deep tracks made landing quite perilous or uncomfortable. The gliders were coming in so fast that we did not have time to clear the field. Some of the gliders bumped into each other as they landed causing further damage and chaos.

At times the saga of the gliders was quite deafening. Then all was quiet for a moment until the cries of the wounded were heard from the wreckage. Some of the gliders fell into enemy area and some landed quite some distance away in the mountains in nearby India. Of the sixty-two gliders only thirty-five reached Broadway. It was soon apparent that it had been a mistake to allow every Dakota to tow two gliders each.

Over twenty men were killed but many more were injured. However over four hundred men, including Brigadier Calvert, and quite a lot of stores, landed intact. The place indeed looked a mess littered with smashed gliders. Nevertheless, as soon as we landed, the soldiers ran as fast as they could to take up their positions. They got all the guns loaded and ready even if the enemy was not actually in sight. There was no shooting, only a bit of understandable uncertainty and panic-stricken worry. The area was actually very quiet, except for the NCOs shouting out orders, 'You go here. This goes there.'

The following morning there was a load of work to be done. The airstrip had to be ready by evening so that the Dakotas could land. We worked hard the whole day in the sun and in the dust, clearing the place of damaged gliders and leveling those awful ditches. Some of the men were cutting down trees, others were sent out to search for survivors. They brought back the wounded and the dead. That evening the Dakotas did land in Broadway. From 5th to 11th March approximately 12,000 men and 3000 pack animals were flown over the jungle far beyond the lines of the enemy.

Meanwhile the plans for the South Staffordshire Regiment were to establish the first 'block'° at Henu Hill°, just south of Mawlu°. We were a Long Range Penetration group, assigned to hold the block at all cost. We were also to send out patrols, many of which I was part of. One British Brigade under Brigadier Bernard Ferguson and one American Brigade of the Merril Marauders° were to walk in from India. It took Brigadier Ferguson a month to get to the area. The Americans however stayed close to Myitkyina in the north to help General Stillwell, the US Commander, to push south.

I met another soldier from the BIC, Freddie Dias. We had a long chat catching up with news. Finally he asked me, 'Steve, (they all called me Steve – some of course called me Charlie) why don't you stay here in Broadway?' I really couldn't as my heart was always with my Staffordshire group. So, on the next day when the Staffordshire Regiment arrived I ran out to meet them. We did not waste time. Our assignment was to block the railway and the road.

Lieut Col. Richards commanded our First Battalion South Staffordshire. He was an experienced infantry soldier, of the quiet type who tolerated an occasional joke. His Column Commander was Major Ron Dess. He too was a fine officer, a thorough soldier in every way. We all took a liking to him.

Floating with the Columns

The Lancashire Fusiliers, the Kings, and the 3/6 Gurkhas were known as the Floating Columns. They floated round the block --approximately around a radius of about 30 miles-- checking, laying ambushes and informing the air pilots of the positions of any Japanese. We, however, raced to a small enemy garrison near Mawlu, on the Mandalay-Myitkyina railway, about fifty miles away from Broadway, which we later named White City --because the tops of the trees were covered with white parachutes that hadn't fallen through with the supplies dropped by Dakotas.

In the meanwhile it was the task of the Royal Engineers from the Lancashire Fusilier Column to blow up the bridge just south of Mohinyin°. We were close by when they blew up the bridge in the early hours of the morning, in a puff of smoke. The whole bridge was cut in half.

As we came to the area, different Platoons were given their positions and instructions about where to go. We were on the right flank of the railway on the hills. *Column 38* was on the left side on the hills and we formed a block. One of our Sections climbed one of the hills and spied the Japanese milling around a small pagoda on top overlooking a paddy field --named Pagoda Hill by the OC. They spotted us and we saw them. There were about a dozen of them. A lot of firing exchanges took place but we couldn't dislodge them from their position. It looked like the Japanese were based at this hill and at the village of Henu.

We then received an order from Brigadier Calvert, who was outside the block area with the Gurkhas. He proposed that Major Ron Dess's *Column 80* of the South Staffordshire Regiment was to charge. 'We're looking for volunteers for the bayonet charge,' he added.

Some of the intelligence section volunteered. I put up my hand and joined the group. We all wanted the experience of killing the first Japanese and getting our adrenaline pumping. We waited –with all our bayonets fixed. The Gurkhas were crawling as they advanced from the other side. We kept the Japanese occupied on this side by firing. Then at dawn we were all to charge down this hill. Meanwhile Capt. Stagg came up to me and said, 'Stephenson, you are not going into this. We need you as our interpreter. We cannot afford to lose you. You will have to stay here and watch.' Reluctantly I had to obey orders, but I managed to get a good view of the battle from O.P. hill.

Then the Sections made a bayonet charge. The Japanese leaped out and charged back. They clashed in the area with our men yelling and shouting as they slashed at the enemy with whatever weapon they had: the Japanese wielding their swords, the Gurkhas fighting ferociously with their kukris. There was hand to hand wrestling as well. Later I heard that Lieutenant George Cairns, who was bayoneted twice, took no heed of his wounds. He shot his assailant, picked up a sword and continued to lead his men. He was awarded a VC° for his brave stand that day. Finally the Japs were driven behind the pagoda. Then there was a pause while both sides lobbed grenades. Unfortunately Lieutenant Cairns died from his wounds later while he was in hospital in India.

Brigadier Calvert's account of the next attack is quite graphic and factual, and does give a picture of what the true situation was. "While I was wondering what the next move was, Freddie came up to me, saluted and said, 'I have two platoons here at your disposal, Sir.' Someone shouted, 'We are short of ammunition.' I immediately thought that if we were short, the Japs must be shorter as they had been fighting longer. The Japs were yelling at us in English, 'You dirty hairy bastards.' So I shouted, 'We will attack as fast as possible in that direction'--pointing towards the enemy-- 'Staffords right, Gurkhas left…When I say the word: Now!' Immediately, all got on their feet and soon the pagoda area was under control."

By the time I was around the hill was ours and we were pursuing the Japs into the village of Henu. There the Gurkhas and South Staffords went into them with their man-pack flame-throwers, burning up at least a dozen more Japs in dug-outs. The remainder fled across the paddy fields. The day ended up with us taking pot shots at them as they ran or crawled away. A few of the Japs who had infiltrated were soon seen off… Freddie's men took over Pagoda Hill.

The bloody battle at Pagoda Hill was won but we had losses: 3 British Officers and 20 of other ranks. There were also the wounded: 4 British Officers and 60 of other ranks.

Landing supplies to White City
Eleven days after fly-in the Special Force's task had been accomplished: both the main road and the rail communication

to the Japanese who were fighting Stilwell had been cut. The garrison was destroyed and this area became known as White City, as the trees around the block were draped with white parachutes which could be seen for miles. Many columns assembled here. The surrounding area was quite beautiful: at the south-east corner was O.P. Hill, from which the platoons had made their charge to Pagoda Hill; to the south there was a stream; the entire area was surrounded by paddy fields, hills and valleys.

Our rations, ammunition and even medicines, all came by parachute --except for a few mule drops and the food for the mules and horses-- they were known as 'free drops'. These drops were most welcome and yet proved fatal if one of the drops fell into a trench where the soldiers lay. Unfortunately sometimes a few soldiers died from these drops. Whenever a Dakota flew past we made sure we were out of harm's way.

We in the Staffordshire group did receive our first airdrop. We prepared fires in the shape of an L. These were land marks for the air pilots to know where to drop the rations. In the airdrop there were barbed wire, K Rations and ammunition. We brought all these supplies to our protected area. Sometimes they fell on treetops. We climbed up, cut them down, and left the parachutes on the trees because it was difficult to remove them. The parachutes were all made of beautiful silk, which must have cost a lot. Nevertheless, those we could untie we brought in. We rolled up the parachutes that were on the ground, brought in all the supplies to the enclosure and then erected a barbed wire perimeter fence around the block. This was very thin and quite inadequate really, and so our supply and ammunition stores weren't really protected enough.

Supplying K Rations

No matter what the conditions were, the soldiers had to be fed. At first the rations, known as the American K Rations, consisted of three packs for a day. They were marked: breakfast, dinner and supper. The packs were in cardboard containers, fully waxed, which was very handy. They could be used as fuel to heat our meals cooked in the mess tin. Each pack contained a small tin of either ham or cheese, for lunch a small bar of chocolate, or a fruit bar, a pack of four cigarettes, a couple of small packets of (not very tasty) biscuits, which you got used to. That was our food and that was all we ate every day. But it was not really enough to sustain a fighting force for a long period of time.

So eventually it was upgraded. We woke up in the morning, opened a small tin of chopped ham and eggs, and had this with our biscuits. We made coffee with a packet of powdered milk and some sugar. In the afternoon we had the same but with cheese in a little tin. For dinner we had pork loaf or corned loaf. At supper there was another pack with bouillon soup. In every pack there were four cigarettes and two packs of biscuits with sugar. On occasions we were given a bonus of caramel sweets well-packed, which we ate with relish. Everyone received seven-day rations, that is, 21 packs of K Rations. During our march we carried this along with a blanket. In addition to this there was our ammunition, our grenades, our rifles, kukris and trenching tools. A load of approximately seventy pounds or more was carried on our backs.

The cigarettes were of toasted tobacco. It was never the same brand in every packet. There was Chesterfield, Old Gold, Lucky Strike and some others. I began the campaign as a non-smoker. The cigarettes were handy for burning off the leeches. I ended up becoming addicted and took up the habit. At times I yearned for my basic food, rice. I managed to get some off the dead Japs, which they carried in a sock.

Chapter 17

Facing danger in War mode

During the night we were given orders to stay in our foxholes as anything moving would be shot at. After two nights the Japs attacked. They attacked on the side of *Column 38*. There was a lot of fighting the whole night, grenades going off, light pistols being shot. The Japanese broke through and penetrated the perimeter with Bangalore Torpedoes˚. A close engagement took place, with several wounded and many killed. It was sad to add that the Battalion Commander Colonel Richards, who had put in a whirlwind counter-attack which he himself had led, had driven out and had then killed many of the enemy, died later from his wounds. He was a nice man, pleasant and accommodating even if a little podgy. At one stage we wondered whether he would be able to keep up with us. We really need not have worried. He was a good trained soldier as fit as any of us. We were sad to lose him. The Second in Command, Major Ron Degg, of *Column 80* then took over as the Battalion Commander.

After a few days, Brigadier Calvert, his body guard Paddy Dermody and Corporal Young went on to Bare Hill, which was supposed to be clear of Japanese. Quite suddenly Paddy

Trophy D'Souza

yelled out, 'Get down!' and pushed the Brigadier down. But Paddy, who was a good friend of mine, was wounded in the groin. When I paid him a visit in the operating trench he said, 'The bastards! I don't want to go out, Charles.' He kept repeating, 'I don't want to go out, Charlie.' I tried to comfort him by saying, 'Paddy, at least you will be going to a hospital in India. They will make you better there. You can fight another day.' He had tears in his eyes and I could see the pain he was suffering. I spoke gently to him again, 'Paddy, when you get to India, please write and tell my Mum that I am well.' He said, 'Charles, I won't forget that.' I didn't have anything to write down the address for him, so I gave it to him verbally, '28 Temple Road, Lahore.'

When he got to hospital in India, gangrene set in. He could not write, so he called a nurse and asked, 'Would you please write a letter to a Mrs. Stephenson in Lahore and tell her that her son is all right.' He asked that his name be put to it (Paddy Dermody) and the name of the hospital he was in. My Mum wrote back to him but he never received it as he had passed away. The Brigadier was most upset about this. I too will miss Paddy very much as, on many occasions during training, he allowed me to ride the Brigadier's horse Jean, a magnificent, white horse.

Paddy was a jockey from Ireland. He was very fond of me and often told me this touching story. While retreating from Burma a Burmese man from the Burma rifles saved him from drowning. Unfortunately in the attempt the man drowned. Paddy always felt that it was his duty to come back and fight for Burma to pay a debt that he owed to one Burman who had saved his life. What a wonderful man he was! He will never be forgotten.

The other Burma Intelligence Corp (BIC) soldier with me was Xavier. On his very first patrol out of the block they ran into an ambush. Xavier was so scared that he froze with fright. He could not retreat with the others but the British soldiers in the group attacked to get him out. They carried him back to the block while he feigned unconsciousness. The whole day he lay with his eyes closed --not eating or making an attempt to speak.

At one stage I saw his eyelids flickering. I gave him a kick and said, 'Get up! Don't put up this act.' He looked at me and said, 'Where am I?' Captain Stagg asked me, 'What do you think we should do, Stephenson?' I replied, 'Sir, if there is a space on the next plane without any wounded to take out, I think he could be sent back.' Xavier was eventually flown out. I have never set eyes on him since my return to the Platoon in India. I don't know if he deserted and to this day I have no idea of his whereabouts.

Another mate of mine, Buck Howell, was born in the West Indies. What a nice guy he was! When I heard that he was wounded, I paid him a visit at the pit. Buck was in tears. 'Charlie, the Japanese have done me,' he said. 'A grenade exploded between my legs.'

I don't know to what extent he was wounded. He was flown out of the block. I met him later in India when they were going to make another attempt to operate on him. All his legs and his private parts were hit --not by shrapnel but by little stones and sand. So he was not very badly hurt but a little disappointed that he was badly wounded and unable to fight.

Chapter 18

Fighting intensely in war mode

By now we were quite accustomed to our new sleeping arrangements. The trenches were lined with the silk parachutes to prevent the sand from falling in, so we had silk sheets to sleep against.

Every night the Japs came from Mawlu and attacked our city from the same position. The north and east sectors of the perimeters were held by the Staffords. The Japs who threw themselves on the barbed wire, tried jumping on each other to bounce over the fence but to no avail. The Staffords fought them off. This particular position was held by Lieut Scholley, a quiet sort of a man. Many of his men kept falling because of the continuous attacks but he promptly had reinforcements flown to his Platoon night after night. As a result of the attacks many young men died while several were wounded.

Major Ron Dess by this time was promoted to Colonel of the Battalion. One day he called Lieut Scholley and asked him, 'Do you want a rest?' His reply was, 'Sir, I was given this position to defend and I'll defend it to the last man.' It was the gallant young officers --brave men, bold, daring, intelligent, and simply the best-- who fought with so many others to give the Chindits a place in history never to be forgotten.

One day I was sent on patrol with a section of men. Our task was to find out where the Japanese were assembled to stage the attacks on the block. The Lance Corporal in charge however was not very smart. We proceeded out of the block and went south through very dense forest. After about 15 miles the men started whining and grumbling and passing remarks that the Lance Corporal did not know where he was heading. As I was his 2nd In-Charge, they approached me to lead them. I told them that he was the leader and that we had to take orders from him.

A little later the Corporal himself approached me and did admit that we were lost. Looking at the map I knew the railway was on our left and suggested we head for this and thus return to the block. My advice was taken and we got back safely using our colored Panic Maps of cloth --which were also used to show our own troops that we belonged to the same group.

The Colonel was not at all pleased with what had transpired and suggested that Captain Stagg lead another patrol immediately. I was pretty tired but after a quick meal five of us set off carrying our automatic guns. We patrolled as far as we could and stopped for the night. We slept together with all our feet together, in the form of a star. Every two hours we woke one another up. It was quite exhausting nerve-wracking but I had learned to stay strong and alert. In fact I think I even looked young for someone eighteen years of age, probably because of the Asian blood in me. The group gave me the last shift of the morning. Captain Stagg however knew that I was tired.

During the night, every two hours we just touched one another or woke one another up, making sure that we did not rustle the leaves in case the enemy heard us. We went a little further and Captain Stagg said, 'You all stay here.' He and the Sergeant went further into an open area, searching with their binoculars for enemy movement. They saw nothing so we came back from that expedition.

On quite a few occasions, the Mustangs° flew over escorting the Dakota planes, bringing our rations and other commodities. They also attacked targets nominated by us or other battalions. On one such mission the Dakotas flew in unescorted to drop parcels for us. Suddenly Japanese Zeros came over and in a few moments most of the Dakotas were shot down.

In spite of the danger the Dakotas were still making airdrops while being shot at and were sometimes getting on fire. I was amazed at the courage of these pilots. The Mustangs returned to remove the enemy from the sky and a dogfight that took place during that time was one of the best I have ever seen. The Japanese lost a few planes and the remainder of their squad sped away. One cannot help feeling sorry for the pilots and the crew of the Dakotas. I felt helpless not being able to do anything from the ground. That helplessness was one of the saddest parts of the war.

There was no sleep in the block as from dusk to dawn every night the Japanese attacked continuously. They fired their Bangalore Torpedoes to blow the barbed wire apart. They used a weapon that made a whizzing effect and used motor bombs as well. During daylight hours, if not on patrol, I would go up to our defense positions, carrying ammunition to replenish the stock required. The scene of battle is never pleasant. I saw hundreds of dead Japanese on the barb wire, with their bodies at different stages of decomposition. To get rid of the stench the dead bodies were burnt with flame throwers. Quick lime was used to cover the dead but this did not help. White city was now also identified by its smell.

Chapter 19

Experiencing new schedules in war mode

Captain Stagg approached me and gave me an order that I was to join the Lancashire Fusiliers, outside the block as the two Burma Intelligence men were wounded and they had no interpreter. Since there was Sergeant Bill Wood, another Burmese Intelligence man in *Column 38*, the Lancashires needed me. It was indeed a very sad day for me to leave this group, the Staffordshire, with whom I had experienced dangerous moments and joyful occasions as well. We had developed a kindred spirit among us. We had become buddies or perhaps something more. We were a brand of brothers.

A light plane with its American pilot was waiting for me outside the block. I entered the plane with a heavy heart. Nevertheless, I greeted the pilot and sat in the seat next to him. He told me the flight would take about 20 minutes. It was one of the scariest experiences I've ever had. I could no longer dwell on the sadness of leaving one's friends behind. I had to face the realities of living dangerously on a war front.

We were flying only about 40 feet off the ground, with big trees looming in front of us. The pilot kept swerving as he flew, not very different from a racing car speeding through a forest, missing the trees just a few feet ahead of us. He sped on, going first left then right then left again and then right, swerving and maneuvering his machine with such skill that I was utterly amazed. It was quite the reality of having one's heart in one's mouth, a hair-raising experience.

The pilot must have noticed how shaken up I was and so, just before landing in an open space, he told me, 'I cannot fly this plane higher as the Japanese would take a pot shot at me.' I was shocked and speechless to know that we had come through such a perilous journey. On landing I was met by a patrol of the Fusiliers and was taken to the Battalion to meet Colonel Christie. The colonel was delighted to see me. After a few days with the column, I was sent for to attend an officers' conference under some trees. The CO gave me a map of the area and pinpointed the area we were in. I was introduced to all the other officers as the BIC (Burma Intelligence Corp) representative and attended all other directives. I felt quite elated about this sudden elevation: a Private, called to a meeting with the top brass.

One day I met a villager who was brought in and who, after interrogation, was found to be safe as a guide. At the meeting the Colonel instructed me to use this villager as a lead to a Brigade rendezvous. I explained this to the Burmese villager, asking him to by-pass the village and go through the jungle. We led the whole column and by dusk got to our destination. At this point I let the villager go on his way. Hacking through the jungle was tedious work as the Burma jungles were entwined with vines that were thick, some of which were the size of a man's thigh. We managed only a mile or two in a day.

Returning to the Regiment

To my good luck we hit the tail end of the South Staffordshire Regiment who had just vacated the block. I was delighted! Now was my chance to join my old regiment again. I walked across with my pack and I went to the South Stafford group and saw all my mates. I asked for Captain Stagg and told him, 'Sir, I joined you in India and I was very happy with you all. But I'm not happy with the Lancashire Fusiliers. Could I come back to you?' He said 'Stephenson, you stay here and I will get a message to Colonel Christie at the Fusiliers.' Since it's a Brigade rendezvous, he could have asked the Brigade to supply another Burma Intelligence Corps man in my place. The fact is I never went back to Colonel Christie.

There's an amazing difference between one Battalion and another. Group dynamics played an important role in army life. It was essential that each section stayed cohesive and that the mate-ship was strong. Captain Stagg was very aware of this. He knew I would function well with the South Staffordshire Regiment. They were bold and daring. They lived to Wingate's motto 'No Surrender'. The officers were of the old school type, where morals and values were important. They fought not to defend but to win. For me the British Army has the greatest fighters in the world. To see them fight is a worthwhile experience: the wounded continuing in battle, fighting to the very end, never giving up. In spite of their terrible wounds battle-wounded soldiers didn't want to leave the army. They wanted to get back to active service once their wounds had healed. The loyalty of the British is commendable. I will fight side by side with the British anytime.

Trophy D'Souza

The monsoon started and the rain pelted down and that made marching a very unpleasant task. The frequent slipping and sliding made the difficult trekking even more laborious because the imprints of the heavier mules' hooves in the mud slowed our progress. Everyone was cursing and swearing, and even the King wasn't spared! We were tired and exhausted and quite nearly frustrated. We had a choice: to keep going or to get left behind --that meant sure death or capture by the enemy. Some of course did end up that way.

Facing a hidden enemy
We were also faced with another 'enemy', leeches. They were everywhere by the thousands. On every little shrub and its branches, as we brushed against the bushes, the leeches stood on the suction side of their bodies waiting to cling on to whatever was passing by. The crafty little creatures got in through the eyelets of our boots and crawled up our legs and sucked away at our blood without our realizing it. After a few minutes it was leech feast day, blood --lovely army blood, healthy fellows' blood-- being sucked away from anyone, everyone! The greedy little leeches drank their fill until they burst. The next thing we knew was that our clothes were saturated with our own blood in several places. Some of the men found leeches on their private parts and bottoms and it made life very uncomfortable and embarrassing for them.

Whenever we had a rest and were allowed to smoke we took the opportunity to burn off these leeches. In fact it was difficult to know which of these three horrible options was the most terrible: the leeches, the Japanese or the mud. To let off steam everyone cursed and swore the whole time. The leeches it seems did not like the lantana bushes and in turn the soldiers did not like the lantana bushes probably because they had prickly leaves and stems. So as we leaned away from these bushes we only brought ourselves nearer to the leeches hanging out to latch on to their helpless victims. Yes, the leeches were on all the other vegetation and kept tagging on to us and draining us of our precious blood.

Chapter 20

Fighting to regain lost ground

After Wingate's fatal trip across the mountains, General Lentaigne took his place. He issued another order for us to capture Mogaung, south of Myitkyina. We had another long march to get there because the Americans and Chinese were having a tough time taking Myitkyina. By this time the South Staffords had trickled down to two companies or a greatly reduced strength, including the reinforcements that had come in. We were all physically and mentally exhausted but the spirit of the British was remarkable. We heard on the grapevine that Brigadier Calvert was not happy with this new order to take Mogaung. Orders, however, were orders and they had to be carried out.

The fighting on the hill
When we reached the hill and the jungles at the opposite side of Sahmaw°, memories came flooding back to 1942 and to the beginning of my trek into India. I was called upon to go on a fighting patrol with the company commanded by Major Nip Hilton. The Major was just five-feet tall, an ex-sergeant-major, bursting with energy. The company consisted of less than a

Trophy D'Souza

Platoon in strength. The rest of the men were wounded or had died in combat. We moved off to try and locate the position of the observation post. Along this pathway running next to the jungle we came to a hill. At that point the Major said, 'Let's go up and check out what there is on top.' The monsoon was at its peak and the heavy rain was slowing us down. Yet we were true to Lord Mountbatten's speech, 'We will fight in the rain.' Our officers kept leading us on.

The hill itself was very steep. Just before reaching the top we came across freshly-dug trenches. We were ordered to form a line and advance a further 20 feet. Just then the Bren Gunner noticed something and came over to inform the Major. Soon everyone panicked and ran down the hill. Major Hilton was still up there and he called out to us, 'Come on up, come on up.'

The heavy rain actually saved us from complete disaster as the Japanese were sitting under a tarpaulin having a drink of green tea with their rifles leaning against the trees. They turned out to be sitting ducks.

The Bren gun opened fire and we started shooting towards that area. Some of the Japs jumped over the other side of the cliff to escape, but there was no chance of survival. You could see huge trees growing out from the side of the mountain and down below there was a deep valley. I grabbed my grenades and when I heard Major Hilton say, 'Throw, throw it,' I threw three grenades that day just to make sure every enemy was down.

Every Jap there was dead. We got the lot. I can't remember the exact number of men there but it must have been at least ten of them, all dead! There was a Jap telephone nearby and it was ringing, I presume whoever was at the other end of the line had heard the shooting and was inquiring about the shots.

One of our men picked up the phone and called out to me, 'Steve you might understand these blokes.'

The person at the other end of the line kept saying, 'Moshy, moshy, moshy.'

I answered, 'Moshy, moshy, my bloody arse! You are all dead.'

Major Hilton spoke to Colonel Degg on the walkie-talkie telling him, 'We got them all.'

It was an observation post and the phone line was to inform their gunners the direction of enemy approach. Major Hilton ordered me to go back to the Battalion in case I was needed. I left with another soldier for Loihinche°, the new base. We carried a couple of Japanese swords and handed them over to the Colonel and were praised with the words, 'Well done! There's no need for you to go back. Stay with the remainder of the Battalion.'

We were tired. We had only half our strength left. Besides, strength-wise in terms of the number of men we had, we had come down to practically one-sixth of our number.

It is worth noting that at every place at which we stopped for the night, on the expedition, we dug a trench. This was compulsory. All we had was a little trench-digging tool: one side like a fork and the other side a digger. Using this tool we dug our trenches. I had to dig many trenches along the way. It's good to remember that all along we had the 65-pound packs on our backs.

Coping with fever at Mogaung

On the outskirts of Mogaung, while walking in Column, I suddenly felt that I was burning with fever. I tried my best to carry on but was feeling weak, sleepy and cold. Then I began shaking like a leaf. I went to the side of the track, removed my bush hat and lay down and closed my eyes. I remember someone trying to give me a hand but I brushed him aside with the words, 'Don't worry, I will join the rear of the column.'

In those days the orders were that if anyone fell behind they were left there. Nobody could cater for another because everyone was exhausted and the law really was 'every man fends for himself.' In the final extreme we had to use our instincts to survive. I was left on this track fast asleep. When I got up it was dark and I still had a high temperature. I looked around and found no one. I said to myself, 'I've got to follow the column.'

Unknown to me, the King's Battalion had sent a patrol looking for Japs. They saw me and thought I was a Jap. They fixed their bayonets and were silently coming towards me. They were going to bayonet me. As they were about to do so I bent down and picked up my bush hat that fortunately was just a foot away. That saved my life. I heard a Corporal call out, 'He's one of us! He's one of us!'

Can you blame them? I was Burmese, a little colored and it was dark. Who was to say I wasn't a Jap? Thanks to that bush hat which saved my life. One of the blokes said to me, 'You nearly fluffed it. We almost gave it to you.'

I was really very sick but I didn't take it all that seriously. I just said I wanted to get to a doctor. They were considerate and said, 'OK. We've just got a little hut a few miles away. We'll take you there.

There was a doctor there and he was operating on some of the wounded of the King's Own

Regiment. They were the ones that had landed in Broadway when I was with them. Some

of them knew me. I went along with them, with one of them carrying my pack and another taking my rifle. When we got to this little hut the MO looked at me and asked, 'What's wrong?'

The men said, 'Sir, he's a B.I.C. from the South Staffordshire Regiment. We found him in the jungle.'

The MO gave one look at me and knew instantly that I had malaria because I was shaking like a leaf. Just then I belched and brought up all that I had eaten --those biscuits and whatever else they had given me. It all came out on the floor. He was pretty annoyed because he was operating and this vomit on the floor made quite a mess of the hut. He told me to clean it up but one of the men said, 'Don't worry, Sir. We'll do it.' They put sand on it and cleaned it up.

The quinine intravenous injection he gave me set me right by the morning, with no more shaking and no temperature. The MO discharged me with, 'You can rejoin your unit now.'

I didn't know where to go. I pulled out the lead pencil from my pocket. We were all given an HB pencil. I broke it in half. In the middle of the pencil was a little compass that showed me the North. Even the buttons on our flaps were all compasses. If you took a button out, it had a slight dent and a little white, creamy dot showing north. If you placed that on the tip of the point of the pencil it would show you North. Anyhow I followed the pencil's path and I knew I was going towards Mogaung. I soon came across tall elephant grass. I must have walked at least a good ten miles by now. I couldn't help saying to myself, 'Oh my God! Do I have to go through all this?'

I started going through this elephant grass very slowly. I fixed my bayonet, put my safety catch forward and began traveling at a snail's pace. Now and again I stopped, trying to listen to sounds around me. My ears were more than alert, ready for any eventuality. My eyes turned sharper than usual and were darting about just about ready for anything. After nearly a mile in this elephant grass I came out on to an opening. Around the opening on the far side, about two to three hundred yards away, I saw a group of men. I said, 'That must be it. But if I go out they might shoot me.'

Waving the Panic Map saves

I went back into the grass, pulled out my Panic Map, and tied it to my bayonet. I came out into the open and shouted. Everyone looked at me. Some immediately ran towards their guns but when they saw the Panic Map they waved me on, 'Come on!' While I was crossing this open paddock almost out of nowhere the Japs opened fire on me from the back, the direction I had come from. I don't know where they were but they were somewhere on a nearby hillock. They kept firing their machine guns but fortunately all their bullets were missing me. The Brits at the other end kept shouting, 'Get down!' I got down at once and had to crawl the next fifty yards on my stomach.

As I was there pulling myself along I lost my Panic Map. I was terribly disappointed. I wanted to go back for it but my mates all said, 'No, let it be. It is better lost.' I was very disheartened about losing the Panic Map because it had the imprint of the north and central part of Burma on it. I also had with me many other souvenirs taken from Jap bodies, e.g. pictures of families, filthy ones, small Japanese flags signed by their relatives and plastic cigarette cases. It was sad to know that they wouldn't be going home with me. Eventually I gave away all the little bits I had collected to friends and some Americans who were delighted to have them.

Due to the shortage of men in both *Column 38* and *Column 80* they were now combined into one. I joined up with Sergeant Bill Wood (BIC). As we were tired we decided to skip digging a trench. We lay under a small bush when the shelling from the Japs commenced. Bill was telling me stories of his young days and all about the Islands South of Burma where he grew up, in Tavoy°. Meanwhile the shells kept falling a little closer to us and we put our heads into the earth to take in the impact. One actually exploded about 3 feet away from us. The bush that we were under disappeared and we heard a thump.

On looking around we saw a friend by the name of Profit, lying in the deep-foot trench he was digging. Bill and I got up, and together with another friend, Farrington, we attended to him. This quiet friend who could just about utter a few words was dead. We tried to lift him out to make the trench deeper but all his guts and liver were falling out. There was no alternative but to bury him in the trench he himself had dug. He was a nice fellow really and I miss him. I visited his grave every time I went to the Taukyan War Grave cemetery in Rangoon, where –whenever I could-- I also always stopped by the graves of my two cousins, and those of Mr. Stagg, Paddy Dermody and many others. We couldn't help but shed tears whenever we remembered them.

Trophy D'Souza

We had only recently heard that Mr. Stagg, our Intelligence Officer, was shot and killed. His batman° (Ernie Blunt) was wounded in the leg. Ernie was with us for quite a few days because there was no clear place to land a light plane to evacuate him. We took it in turns to carry him on the stretcher. The poor guy was in terrible pain. He cried and told me that he did not want to die. He was a tall, strapping man and very good looking too. A few days later, however, he succumbed to his injuries. If we only had helicopters in those days I am sure many lives would have been saved.

Field Marshall Wavel also had his son, a Captain, sent to the Battalion, earlier in the expedition, as one of those in the Reinforcement. Unfortunately he was wounded and I was told that just the skin of one of his hands was holding on to a wrist. He refused to be evacuated and said, 'There are many other soldiers also needing treatment. I'll wait my turn.'

These were the type of officers and men of the British army. They were strong-willed and tough fighters. However, there was an order from the FM to Brigadier Calvert that his son had to be on the next plane. Accordingly Brigadier Calvert ordered his son to comply.

After the capture of Mogaung, Myitkyina had still not fallen to the Americans. While we were waiting for further orders we saw some Chinese soldiers passing us going south. They carried huge cooking pots on their heads. Seeing how casual they were we too began to relax and just wait.

No stopping at Myitkyina

Then the orders for us to move came. We had to bypass Myitkyina and get to Shaduzup°, where hopefully some planes would be waiting to fly us out. It was quite a scramble. With the last bursts of energy left in us, everyone pushed himself to get there. It was quite disorderly. When we got there after about a two-hour march, we found no planes. That meant we had to go on further to Warazup°. This time the planes were there waiting for us and so was the American field kitchen, with hot food. We enjoyed that meal, which proved to be a banquet for us, sumptuous and plentiful. After a little rest we boarded the planes that took us to India.

I remember the few of us left in the Battalion, just under 200 men, queuing up for a medical.

We were told to strip off, while the MO walked down the line, examining each one. Some had to be hospitalized. I had a few cuts on my legs and some leech bites that had turned septic, which was really not too bad. We got towels and went for our first showers in nearly six months. Here, after the campaign was over, we received our Chindit shoulder badges and Certificates. We were delighted and proud to be part of a Special Force that had operated behind enemy lines.

On orders to return to BIC Headquarters in Circular Road in Calcutta, Bill and I went to wish Colonel Ron Dess and the other officers. It was sad leaving the friends we had made: Bob Allen, Farrington, Corporal Stanley and another two friends. At the station, we met some other BIC friends who were attached to other Battalions. We were given a new set of uniforms (Baggy Greens), money that we never received while behind the enemy lines and a Second-Class train warrant. We were also given four weeks' leave. I went shopping, bought myself a fitting pair of green trousers and caught the train to Lahore.

Trophy D'Souza

There is always a hassle about getting to travel on trains in India but this time I managed alright. Eventually, when I got to Lahore, all my troubles seemed so far away. Mum and my brothers and sisters were very happy to see me. Of course, I was really kept busy, as I had to keep telling them of the many experiences I'd had in the months that had gone by. In the course of conversation Mum told me that she had received a letter from Paddy Dermody and had replied to him, wishing him well.

I had to break the news to her that he had died of his wounds, after gangrene had set in. She was shocked and just sat in silence for a few moments trying to take it all in. Mum was very proud of my achievements, of the uniform I wore, the one stripe I had, the Chindit Badge and the letter of commendation from General Lentaigne. I gave them to her for safe keeping. In 1954 when I got married, Mum passed all these items on to my wife Daphne. They are still in our possession.

Chapter 21

Coping with routines of war and rest

After 4 weeks of holidays we all had to report back to Mhow. All we did there was PT in the morning with no parades or guard duties. We spent most of the time just relaxing, taking it easy in order to help us recuperate. We were given Special Food –e.g. cutlets, roast, soups, porridge, eggs etc. We were the envy of many of the other soldiers there. Now and again I would take some extra helpings and pass them on to my friends George King (known better as King George) and Charlie Walmsley.

These good days never lasted very long, for after a month we were back in Jhansi (in northern India), training for another expedition behind the lines in the Maymyo area. This time instead of having BIC attached to a Battalion, we had a full Section, including a Captain, Albert James Terry. It so happened that we were attached to the First Battalion South Staffordshire Regiment. I was delighted but soon found out that all the men had changed. The old hands had been sent back home to England. There was one surprise in the whole Battalion. I met Buck Howells again and we had a few laughs together. I remember walking behind this mule in the slush and mud, and every time it urinated its fanny would flip in and out and friends would say to me, 'Steve, it's winking at you.'

We BIC boys were a fully-trained group who had all seen action. Around Christmas the Colonel granted us a ten-day holiday. When we returned, we found that the expedition had been cancelled and that we had to report to BIC Headquarters in Calcutta. Mandalay had fallen and *Division 17* was now attacking Meiktila°. We were loaded into trucks and immediately went straight down through all those hairpin bends. We were needed urgently by various Battalions. Oscar O'Hara and I were sent to the First Battalion West Yorks. Colonel Cooper was the CO and their adjutant was a person of mixed parentage.

Bringing back Thazi memories

I knew the Meiktila area quite well, having lived for so many years in Thazi, which was approximately just 20 miles away from there. I was excited and looked forward to this more comfortable way of advancing by transport. Unknown to me, however, was the fact that now we were attacking the enemy and not just defending premises or avoiding confrontation. A few days later my Platoon Commander, Major Luthenbraine, informed me that my first cousin, Wilfred Stephenson, had died in action when a shell had exploded near him. Wilfred's father was my Dad's younger brother.

We captured Meiktila and spent a few days there, near the lakes. We got on the trucks again and pushed forward past Thazi before crossing the railway. It brought back many memories of my catapult days as a young boy. While advancing down the Rangoon-Mandalay road we stopped off at the township of Pyawbwe°. I was sent on a fighting patrol with 'B' Company. Major Digby was the Company Commander. We were going through a paddy field towards quite a big village when we came across a Phongyi (Buddist Monk). I was called to interrogate him and he assured me that there were no Japs in the village, so we carried on further. Just then one of those in our group shouted out, 'Japs'. The whole company was caught in the middle of the paddy field. I looked around for the Phongyi but he had disappeared.

At that moment I felt tricked and would have shot him. They were sniping at us from treetops, with bullets whizzing past us in showers. One of our men was shot dead and his mate who went to get him out was also shot. The Platoon Lieutenant with another man did try to get them out and they too were killed on the spot. Bullets were flying all around us and we had to take cover behind the ridges of the paddy fields. Major Digby wanted to try and recover the bodies of the four killed but I advised him not to do so. While we were running back from where we had come purely for cover, the Japs were having a field day. Many of our company were wounded. The person in front of me was hit as well. Stevenson, the Company Sergeant Major, was also wounded as well as my mate Oscar O'Hara who was waiting to give me a cup of tea. Oscar said with a sigh of relief, 'Thank the Lord you made it.' The ambush lasted more than half the day.

When we got out the big guns opened up and the Japs scattered. From the top of this slight rise we picked them all with our machine guns It was then that I got another sad message from Divisional Headquarters that another first cousin of mine, Malcolm Taylor (Dad's sister's son), was tied to a tree with another officer and bayoneted in several places. Malcolm had just got married to an Anglo Indian girl about 10 days before being sent in. He died near the township of Pyu°. Further down the road, Oscar and I went on another fighting patrol, this time with Colonel Cooper. His adjutant was there too.

There was a lot of fighting on both sides, with bullets whizzing past and mortar bombs dropping everywhere. The two of us were near the Colonel and as the bombs got nearer, I told Oscar to get behind this tree. We did so, and our lives were saved. The Colonel and his adjutant both died in that attack. There's so much that happens in war that is due to luck or due to what Christians believe is Providence, or God's care, or because of the prayers of others for us. In humanistic terms we literally live to fight another day! Whatever may have been the situation the actions and constant patrols, not forgetting the walk through the Hukaung Valley, began to wear me down from the brave strong man I once was, who had set out like 'superman' into this war adventure. Physically I was exhausted and must admit I had nearly become a nervous wreck too. I badly needed a break. Just a week off would have done me a world of good. But in a war situation is it realistically possible to get any respite?

The break came somewhere between our assignments at Pyinmana° and Toungoo°. Meanwhile I had a personal problem. I had this grinder in my mouth which looked bad and black too. There was no pain, and though it had been there in that condition for the last few years I decided to do something about it right then. So I made this excuse of a toothache and got sent to Divisional Headquarters to see a dentist. On the next morning I could only see a medical surgeon not a dentist. Without any anesthetics he began to extract this tooth. He pulled and tugged but to no avail. Finally he had to crush it and then pulled it out in little bits. Can you imagine the pain I went through? My face swelled up like a balloon. I did get my week off but regretted asking to see a dentist. Two years down the line I was still pulling out bits of that tooth.

Chapter 22

Facing the moment of truth

I rejoined the Battalion and we continued our push south. After a few small skirmishes we reached Nyaunglebin°. We camped at the Railway Station for a few days. One day, I heard a shout from one of the Burmese soldiers, 'Barama, Burma. Steve, Dekko! See Burma-wallah outside our perimeter.' It brought a smile to my face. I called the Burmese man in for interrogation and reported my findings to the Commanding Officer. The news was that a few miles down the road, and about 500 yards up a dirt cart track, there were about 1000 Japs. The CO immediately called a Company Commanders' conference, one that I attended quite often. All British Commanders appeared to think that the figures (of enemy numbers especially) that were reported were exaggerated.

His report began with these words, 'The information received through our Intelligence Corporal, I believe, is that there are about 500 Japs not far from us.' I was quite stunned at the reduced number quoted. He continued, 'I would therefore like to dispatch a company to attack them. Major Adams 'A' Company, together with Corporal Stephenson must proceed. The guide will lead the way.' I went back to the 'A' Company with the Major. He then called for a Platoon Commanders' meeting and informed them that there were about 250 Japanese down the road and that we would be going in as soon as possible. (Notice the further reduction in numbers quoted.) I tried to explain that the report didn't mention or suggest the actual numbers that were first spotted, but it was to no avail. The guide and I got into the first truck and on orders moved off.

At the designated spot we all got out and prepared ourselves to go up this gradient of a cart track, which on both sides was covered with thick impenetrable prickly bamboo, quite impossible to go through. As we commenced our climb I noticed a wire on the left side of the track carefully hidden away in the bamboo thicket. I reported this to the Platoon Commander who suggested we explore this. We traced the wire down to the road, to a Japanese telephone. I questioned the guide again to check if he was leading us into an ambush. He assured me that he only saw them while passing along in his bullock cart. The Company Commander said, 'We will carry on.' Actually as we were on a gradient the Japanese in their hideout on another hilltop could see us through the bamboo thicket that we moved along.

While we were continuing along the grooves made by the carts, between two hillocks on either side of the track, the guide stopped me and told me to look around the one on the left. I did so and could quite clearly see the Japanese sitting in their trenches. The forward section got to this point together with the Platoon Commander. The Company Commander followed but was eager to know the reason we were delaying the trek. Soon the orders went through and Bren guns and small arms fire opened up on the Japanese position. However, we were all cramped in the small area between these two hillocks and I felt very uncomfortable and insecure on the left hand side.

After firing a few rounds from my rifle, I decided to move to the right side of the track. It was not long before I got there when the Japanese opened up with all their machine guns blazing. All we could do was to put our heads down. Then disaster struck. There were two direct hits on our position by mortar bombs. We got orders to pull back. Everyone that could run back did so but the Japanese saw us through the bamboo thicket and opened up on everyone that darted across. I hesitated but soon got this push from the Company Commander, 'Go.' Bullets flew past but I escaped.

War taking its toll

Rejoining the Company at the other end we discovered that we had lost four men and had a few wounded ones, including the Company Commander. I was not injured in any way but was shaking like a leaf for about 2 hours. I was truly shell-shocked. I gained control of myself by just talking to myself. Even today I show effects of that nightmarish experience and appear timid and diffident at certain moments. The fact is that the war has damaged my nerves. The trembling on that day was worse than what one experiences in a malaria attack. My teeth were chattering and my whole body was trembling, and of course the tears just kept flowing. It was really one of the most terrible experiences I've had. The guide next to me was bleeding in the cheek as he continued to run towards the Jap positions. I presumed that he had an agreement that he would just have to lead us to that spot. We threw down some smoke bombs as a camouflage and then got out the bodies of those killed.

A message was sent to the gunners, who opened up. Meanwhile, we got into our trucks and went back to the Battalion. I was still shell-shocked and never spoke to anyone about what had happened. It took a few days before I could tell Oscar of my ordeal. Whenever I speak about these attacks tears just keep flowing as the memories flash back in frightening sequences. The Japs now began leaving Rangoon as the only way out for them was to come up north to Pegu°. In that way, they could cross the River Salween to Moulmein onto Thanbyuzayat° through the Death Railway and into Bangkok. To thwart this move the 17th Division° was racing to get to Rangoon first to cut off the Japanese from crossing the road East to West. We were in fact the Black Cat Division° that retreated from Burma and were now eager to be the first to re-take it.

When we got to Pegu, which is about 40 miles (app 65 km) from Rangoon, we came across our Prisoners of War, some of those who had worked on the Death Railway (Australians, Americans and English). Some of them were in a terrible state. Others who had been reduced to skin and bones were literally on their last legs. A few of them could not even stand up. We were asked to give up one of our blankets for their comfort. We also learned that Lord Louis Mountbatten was arranging to make a spectacular landing by sea to capture the Capital. To stop him doing this we raced down the road encountering a few skirmishes. We got to Htaukyan (2 hours from Rangoon) and heard that there were no Japanese in

Rangoon. The Division was not allowed to advance anymore and had to return to Pegu.

Lord Mountbatten's landing took place fortunately with no shots fired. Even the prisoners had climbed the roof of the Rangoon Jail and displayed a sign saying that the Japanese had gone. After the bombing of Hiroshima and Nagasaki (6th & 9th August, 1945), with atom bombs, the Japanese surrendered. Leaflets to this effect in Japanese were dropped all over Burma, inviting Japanese troops to give themselves up. Many did not want to do so and some never got the message, so a few Japanese died or were killed unnecessarily.

Our job as interpreters however was not yet over. I was called upon to go on a patrol in the Pegu area with Lieutenant Powell and his Platoon, chasing a dacoit gang headed by Aung Ban Pyu, who was said to be terrorizing some villages. The Burmese Police accompanied us. We got to this village along a track from Tanathpin°. We contacted the headman and asked that all the men of the village attend a meeting. The police were rather cruel and made the men raise their arms shoulder high. Only when they produced some type of weapon were they allowed to sit down. Many homemade weapons were found but nothing modern. Lieutenant Powell was quite annoyed with this type of bullying by the police and told the men to put their hands down and to go back to their homes.

Chapter 23

Seeing the softer side of war

Meanwhile, I came across one of the many wives of Aung Ban Pyu and took her to the Platoon Headquarters. She began crying when she had to face up to us army personnel. She was a very pretty lady, charming and reserved in her own way. I put my hand on her shoulder to console her (which is not really allowed in the Burmese tradition, where no touching is permissible). I informed her that we intended to keep her till we could hear from her husband. Yet all she did was sob continuously. I sent for the headman and told him that Aung Ban Pyu would have to surrender with all his arms and men before we could release his wife. His reply was, 'I'll see what can be done.'

After a day he came back to me saying that Aung Ban Pyu would surrender at 10:00 am the following day. Early in the morning that day Lieutenant Powell placed his men in position in case of an attack. In a distance we saw the column of the dacoit men with their guns approaching the village. They came in and laid their weapons on the ground. The Police tied their hands behind their backs and kept them in custody. Pyu then spoke briefly to his wife in his tribal Mon language which I did not understand. She in turn replied, glancing at me a few times somewhat nervously, as she conversed with her husband. We then allowed her to return to her home.

Aung Ban Pyu told me in Burmese that he had brought his men, with all their weapons, to surrender. He said that he had no intention of escaping and asked if I would kindly get permission for him to spend the night with his wife, also mentioning that he wouldn't forget my kindness.

I translated his request to Lieutenant Powell, who threw the onus back onto me, 'What do you think?'

I said, 'Sir, it's up to you.' I had no intentions of wanting to rush into any answer. I did not want to be responsible for any decision in the matter.

He thought for a few minutes and then said, 'OK, let him go. We'll keep the other men of his with us.'

The next morning there was no sign of Aung Ban Pyu, his wife or the headman. The prisoners were taken over by the police and we rejoined the Battalion. The Colonel was not happy about the escape of their leader and also about letting him sleep out. At the Battalion I was quite proud about what I had achieved in the surrender of the dacoits and showed off the pistol I got for my troubles. Tired and exhausted I put the gun under my pillow and was soundly asleep in a few minutes. In the morning the gun was missing. I was pretty sure a Brit must have stolen it. All I could do was curse him. I should have reported this, but did not do so.

Our 'C' Company was dispatched to a very big village called Minywa° stationed on one of the tributaries of River Salween. At this place we were ordered to destroy most of our grenades. While there I heard a roaring noise that kept getting louder by the minute. I made quick enquiries of the local people who informed me that everyday at this time, around 3 pm, the water would roll down in one big wave. In doing so it would rise to its maximum capacity. This gave me the idea of how to get rid of some of our grenades. After the deluge I would line up about 10 of our Platoon on the bridge, lob a couple of grenades into the river and call out to grab the fish that popped up before they could recover from the blasts. So, for the six weeks that we were there, every Friday, we had fish for dinner. It suddenly became a most enjoyable time for all soldiers.

There were also a lot of Pwe° concerts with Burmese dancing girls in the limelight. The dancers in this form of Burmese drama attracted crowds and reflected some of the finer points of Burmese culture. Attending a Pwe show was also one of those aspects of life that mattered in social circles. The troops were expected to throw money to these girls if they liked the performance.

Another exciting day for me was a trip to the town of Kawkareik°, with Major Ormsby and a section of men on an army truck. The whole town was decorated with paper streamers and the people were all dressed in bright colorful sarongs. As we approached the archway, there was a lot of clapping, singing and Burmese dancing. We were stopped at the town hall. We got off our truck and found the Japanese soldiers (who had now surrendered), showing their respects to us by bowing. We were invited into the hall by them and they sat at this long table on the opposite side. On the table was all their weaponry and ammunition including seven Japanese swords. Everything was sparkling and well displayed. Outside, the dancing and beating of the drums was still going on.

Chapter 24

Dealing with the surrender

Major Ormsby informed the Japanese Commander that we were only an advance party to see that all was in order for the official surrender, which was to take place the next day. The Major and I went out to the joyful commotion. He knew how to assert his authority, and as soon as he put up his hand there was silence immediately. I did the translation of what he had to say. 'Thank you all for coming and for your support. We are of the Black Cat Division° that retreated from Burma but we are now back.' (Plenty of clapping) 'Tomorrow will be the signing date of the Japanese surrender in your township. Please give your support to the Colonel and his staff'.' With this he removed his shoulder badge of the Black Cat and pinned it on one of the officials present.

We both walked amongst the people and there was plenty of handshaking and pats on the back. All this excitement gave one goose bumps. You felt proud that you also were one of those that took part in the action that gave people their independence and freedom. We boarded our truck and returned to the Battalion, now stationed alongside the Mudon Lakes°. The inscription in the impressive Kohima (in Nagaland, India) memorial truly resonated on that day: *'When you go home tell them that for their tomorrow we gave our today.'* These great words were wonderful feelings which we too felt on a day like that.

One day the Battalion Colonel called me and showed me two round balls 6 inches in diameter, brass-looking objects. They were very heavy and since I did not know what they were, he told me to throw them away in the lake. As I walked towards the lake with them he stopped me and called me back, and said that he might use them as paper weights. He then asked me to go down to the town and bring back a jeweler. He also told me not to mention this to the sentries at the gate. I had to give some excuse to them to explain why the jewelers were around. I did what I was told and returned.

The first question the Colonel asked me to find out was what those two balls were. I found out about them from my enquiries and then informed the CO that they were gold. He then gave me a packet of stones and asked me to get the contents separated, diamonds from zircons. There were quite a few stones clustered together. With a pincer the jeweler and I sat down to the job. The Colonel meanwhile was pacing outside the tent in case anyone might come to see him or in case someone suspected something not quite proper was going on. The jeweler told me I could help myself to a few stones and that no one would know anything about it. There were pink, yellow and white diamonds. I was tempted but never took any. I wrapped them up and marked them on the outside of the paper packet and gave them back to the Colonel. Why the sorting? I don't know. The gold and stones were taken out of rings confiscated by the Japanese.

We went on a few more patrols by boat, visiting outlying villages. On one such expedition we happened to sleep the night in a bamboo-made hut. In the early hours of the morning, while dressing, Major Ormsby pulled on his boots and was stung by a scorpion. We had to spend another few days there mainly to look after him. We were able to arrange for food from the village.

On another occasion we spotted a lone Japanese wandering about dazed. He must have been sick. We found him asleep on the concrete slabs near a pagoda. We noticed grenades and ammunition around his body so we surrounded him. As soon as he started to stir one of our men shot him. It was a horrible scene, and the memory of it still haunts me. I felt we could easily have disarmed him and then questioned him later. I still just can't understand why we killed him. I still get up some nights in a fright just thinking of the incident. I realize that my hat saved me from a similar situation and am grateful to God for His care and protection.

On returning to the Battalion the BIC Quarter Master rolled up in a jeep and took me away to the BIC Platoon Headquarters in Moulmein. We had a nice time there, holding a few parties with the local people.

The building of Death Railway

After about 2 months in Moulmein, I was ordered to proceed with Captain Tony Vertannes, Sergeant Bill Wood and Corporal Clifford Dixon to the Railway of Death. This railway was built by the prisoners of war, who were mostly Australian, British and Americans, all of them captured in Singapore. The Railway extended from Thanbyuzayat in Burma to Bangkok

Trophy D'Souza

in Thailand (then known as Siam). Our job was to play the role of Custom Officers but it turned out to be anything but that. We were rather surprised to find so many wooden bridges along the way, all coming upwards from the valley below, held up by small logs or slabs of wood placed in a crisscross fashion which were meant to stabilize the bridge. It was an amazing fete of engineering by the prisoners, given the lack of materials and equipment available during war.

Clifford and I were then dropped off at Apalon° station while Captain Tony and Bill carried on to Neeky°, closer to Bangkok. I believe they had a ball there. We were given quarters in one of the prisoner's huts and the Japanese supplied us with our food. All the Japs ate was sweet boiled rice and a few leaves and plain tea to wash it down. Apalon was just a jungle station with no houses or village people. Twice a day we would go down to the station, to attend the arrival of the trains. The Japanese would see us coming and would line up and bow to us in their traditional style. I felt a little apprehensive about this but surmised that they did this because we were the conquerors. However I didn't really know if we could trust them as they had treated their own Prisoners of War earlier so badly.

Understanding the enemy

As a 20-year-old soldier I did take advantage of the situation, sticking my chest out and checking out the parade in front of me. One day I thought I'd have a chat with the Japanese Commander, Major Tumariya. I found him to be a very nice man. He taught me many Japanese words and even a song (Miyota Kaino), which I still know. I even took him out shooting in the jungle. He once stopped me from shooting a Black Panther, which was only 20 feet from me, for no plausible explanation. To add to the sweet Japanese food provided to us, I shot many a deer and wild fowl that we added to our menu, which we willingly shared with the Japs.

On one occasion I warned the Major about one of his Kempetai men, prowling near my hut, telling him that if I saw him again I would kill him. During this time I visited Captain Tony Vertannes and Bill Wood at Neeky, near the 3 Pagoda Pass, not too far from us, on many occasions.

After 2 months I was recalled to Moulmein. I was not long there, when I was ordered to take some Indian prisoners down to Rangoon. These guys had apparently collaborated with the Japanese. As I was the only one with about 10 of them I refused to take the responsibility of any escape, which was agreed to by the CSM French. When we slept for the night in Pegu the leader of this group ran away. I reported this in Rangoon to the Administration Command (South East Asia) and was nearly reprimanded. I had to make quite a few telephone calls to get exonerated.

I met my second eldest sister Madge there. She was on RSM° for the WACI°. I presume that for all my good work I was sent on holiday back to Lahore to assist in my family's return to Rangoon. When I got there, they had already left for Calcutta to board a ship back to Rangoon. I got a troop ship from Calcutta and returned to Rangoon to find that my name was on the notice board to attend the Victory Parade in London. The three other men whose names were on had already left. So I had missed out: one more disappointment to a string of others earlier.

Trophy D'Souza

I was 21 years old by now and was sent to do an apprentice course in the Irrawaddy Flotilla Company. I did not like the job as it was too complicated for me. I had to attend drawing classes and other classes. I had long forgotten how to sit on classroom benches and how to stay attentive at academic work. I think I was more of the practical type –catapults and canons. I packed it in and joined one of the two LCT's smuggling rice from Burma to Karimoon Island (near Singapore). I did only one trip and found that too quite boring and uneventful.

Getting disembodied and surviving

I received my disembodiment Certificate (i.e. release from the Army) on the 31st May 1946 after serving 5 years with the Colors. I felt proud of all my achievements but was not happy with the way I was discharged. We had to line up to see an Indian Accountant for any balance of money due to us. When you got to him he would pull out a few sheets of paper with your name on it and rattle off in Bengali counting the total given and the balance owed to you. In my case for example, the amount was Rs. 300/. I refused to accept that and he counted the balance again and this time it went up to Rs. 650/. I again refused the amount. The total finally went up to Rs. 900/- With disgust I accepted the amount. I knew that I was due much more than that because on many occasions during the war, I was without a pay-book, and so got nothing. The British guys ended with a suit and a handshake while we (non-Brits) of the same rank got nothing special. We (KA BYAS) Anglos were the forgotten ones.

The continuing medical facilities that were due to us at the end of the war, at that time in Burma, were not provided to us. We were the forgotten and neglected BORs. Those who could show they had British ancestry managed to get British Citizenship. Those who could not prove it due to papers being lost during the war are now dead or are still struggling to survive in Burma, after giving up the best part of their lives to fight for King and the British Empire. So, was it really worth it all for many of us? We were all the loyal subjects left to our own destinations. The lucky ones like us managed to emigrate on British Passports. But even living in Australia does not qualify us for any extra facilities like the Australian Veteran's Gold Card. I just about survive on my pension alone from which I continue to pay for my private medicals too.

Out of pure interest in all things military I joined the Burma Army for a short period. I tried to train some batches of new recruits but found that on many occasions they formed little groups and developed behavior patterns not very similar to those of dacoits pilfering in the villages. At one time I had evidence to show they had wanted to knock me off as well, probably because I was too demanding. I was disappointed with their performance and when the opportunity came I left the job. It was then that I started to worry: I had no job and no education.

Just then I chanced to meet a friend on the road with whom I got chatting about all things Burmese and about the War. He asked me to see an ex-Captain Adams from the Fifth Field Battery. I had heard of the man and of his many connections. I wasted no time and got to see him. Adams gave me a note to contact a Mr. Thomas Holmes of Fair Weather Richards & Co.

Trophy D'Souza

Daphne Jones, who lived down stairs in my building, was Mr. Holmes' secretary. I spoke to her briefly telling her I wanted to see Holmes. With her help I did get to see Mr. Holmes. He asked me to come back the next day to meet a Mr. Findlay, the manager of the King Island Rubber Plantation in Mergui°. Mr. Holmes, without telling me, spoke to Daphne to ask her what she thought of me. Daphne probably tried to be professional about it and told him that she didn't think I'd be suitable for the job. Situations change and people change in life, and it is indeed surprising that many years later, in 1954, I married this very same lady, Daphne.

Chapter 25

Coping with new experiences

I saw Mr. Findlay and got the job as an apprentice rubber planter. The job itself was not difficult. It entailed walking around the estate and checking on the rubber tappers, as there was a lot of pilfering of latex taking place. The tappers would put tins into the ground, cover them with leaves and fill them up. When everyone went back to the factory, some other person (apparently a contact, outside the tappers' group) would collect these tins from the hole. In this way they got more money. Looking back on the pilfering, one does not feel one can really blame them, as they were paid peanuts. Anyhow, one of the overseers reported a tapper to me and showed me the spot with the tin and latex in it. When the man came to the factory I had no alternative but to sack him.

I was now on the Plantation for over a year and quite enjoyed my open life here, with a bungalow and a servant to do my cooking. One day some communist (maybe trade union) guys came on to the island to stay. They took Mr. Findlay away for a ransom and called a meeting of all the staff. They informed me that I had wrongly sacked a tapper and they got to the bottom of the whole story. They went so far as to behead the overseer, Mg Thein, because he had issued threats against them. The situation soon got much more complicated and so I decided to leave. I told Paddy Webster, Assistant Manager, of my decision and he reluctantly agreed. I was given a lot of papers to give Mr. Ferguson at FR's. To leave the island I had to bluff my way out telling them that I was going to Merqui for toilet requisites and other purchases.

I bought my plane ticket to Rangoon hoping I'd get away from it all but noticed that even here there was some uneasiness in the city in business circles and in general civil administration. With the War just over and with all that I had endured through it I had begun to lose my bearings somewhat. I was now a very nervous and timid person and even today I still show this lack of self-confidence. The situation in Rangoon had indeed changed and added to the tensions one had to face.

One day, with my shorts and canvas shoes on I decided to see Mr. Ferguson, the manager. This is how he greeted me. '*Kya Mungtha Hai*,' in Hindi. (What do you want?)

I replied in English and told him I was from King Island. He appeared friendly at first and said, 'Sit down.'

I handed him the official papers I'd brought along and told him that I'd resigned. Then his whole attitude changed. Basically he told me that there was no leave pay or severance pay-out. I left with nothing. That is how some of the British managers treated people.

Living in the slow lane
I was now 27 years old with no work, no qualifications, and no education. Mum said to me, 'You can stay here and eat here, but don't ask me for money.' I never did.

There was not much room in the flat at our place in Brooking Street, in the heart of town, and all the beds were occupied, I slept on the floor in the sitting room.

My elder sister Madge who was married came over one day and asked me, 'When are you going to get a job?' It wasn't something that I hadn't thought about but how did I have to go about it? I never had any idea of what I could do. Moreover I had no self esteem or motivation left in me. What would I do? I kept thinking about it for a few days and all I ended up with was a blank screen. Then someone somewhere must have been praying for me because, one day, after hearing what I believe was a voice I decided to pray.

Every morning I went to Mass at the Cathedral, after which I would stay back for a few minutes, talk to Our Lady begging her for help. Tears would come into my eyes as I pleaded for guidance. After a few visits, one morning, I came out of the church and walked along Montgomery Road, quite aimlessly. I must have done about 3 miles before I decided to go down a street that had a cloth shop. I can't explain why but I decided to walk in. I saw an Indian man looking at samples of cloth that had been brought in by a salesman from another country.

When I had got the man's attention, he looked up at me. I then asked him, 'Do you know of any jobs going?'

He replied, 'Sorry, no jobs here.'

Another gentleman who happened to be there in the shop heard me and then tapped me on the shoulder and said, 'Lad, you're looking for a job?'

'Yes, Sir, I am,' I replied.

He pulled out his visiting card and told me to see him at the Strand Hotel the next day at 9 am. I walked back home, excited that something had finally begun to happen, even if I hadn't yet struck gold.

Testing times with Inspection tasks
At home I owned a rayon pair of trousers that crushed easily, a cream-colored long-sleeved shirt and a maroon-colored tie. I ironed these and kept them ready. I arrived at the Strand Hotel at 9 the next morning. Mr. David (a Jewish business man) was waiting for me. Together we walked down to the Chartered Bank Building into the lift. Then we went along a corridor and up a flight of stairs into the office of the International Inspection and Testing Corporation. I was introduced to the Manager, Alex D'Lorenzo. Mr. David introduced me to Alex and then left. The first question that Alex asked me was, 'How much do you want per month?'

I'd never before heard an employer ask such a question. It stunned me for a while and when I could get my thoughts back I replied, 'Whatever you wish to give me, I shall be grateful.' He started me on Kyats 300/-, which at that time was quite a good salary, approximately $300 in today's money. I was to commence work the next day.

I got home quite excited and told mum about it. All she said was, 'Son, only when you bring home the first pay packet will I believe you.'

I was very nervous because of my lack of education and because I did not know what the job was about. After ironing my clothes again the next morning I went to work. Alex asked me to share his desk and to write a letter to the President of the organization on some business issues. I was stuck for words. I'd never written a business letter in my life. In any case my grammar was terrible and my vocabulary limited. What was I to do? Maybe it was someone again who was praying for me. My inspiration went into over-drive because God must have stepped in.

I went down to the Burma Chamber of Commerce, where some of the girls I knew worked, and asked them for help. They more than obliged. Alex had some appointments and went off. I copied this draft and gave it to the secretary to type. When Alex read it he was quite pleased and the letter was sent to the Company President Mr. Frank Rizzo (American) in Tokyo, Japan. Meanwhile I went down to the Newsagent and purchased a book on letter writing. At the same time I began finding out more about the work of the company, which was about Inspection (of rice, pulses and beans, purchased by foreign countries), and about Insurance (i.e. damage to goods coming into the country).

Four months later, Alex told me that he was on his way to Bangkok and asked if I would look after the office and staff while he was away. He also told me that if there were any letters I should reply to them. He then wrote to me a little later to tell me that he had resigned. It was as if the whole world had collapsed on me. Here was I, unfamiliar with the work, with 12 office staff, a bunch of outdoor staff, not skilled in language or business skills running a company. To add to it I was awaiting the arrival of the Okinawa Trade Mission headed by Mr. Nashiro. However, everything just worked out. I got a letter appointing me as Manager and Director of the Company. I wrote back saying that I could not do the job on that salary. So they raised it to Kyats1200 per month which was quite a reasonable Manager's salary in those days.

Chapter 26

Starting life again – new avenues

It was only then, with some sort of a package in hand, that I could approach Daphne, whom I was in love with, to ask for her hand in marriage. Her answer was that I should ask her mum and dad. I of course did so. So, after 7 years of chasing her, we are now together for nearly 60 years. With the Grace of God I hope to reach the magic 60 years, thanks to Daphne who taught me so much that I needed to know in business and in life. She truly helped me become a more balanced person and gently corrected me of many the faults I had. She was like a guiding star to me. Were it not for her I might have lost my way in life. I owe it all to Daphne.

We bought our first brand new car, the A40, with a loan from her father. Early on in our marriage, Daphne suggested we both do a full medical. We did this at the Seventh Day Hospital in Rangoon and to our disappointment found out that my sperm was not strong enough to produce any kids. In those days in Burma, they never advised us as to how to deal with this sort of a situation. Maybe the local doctors didn't have the know-how then.

Trophy D'Souza

On another occasion Daphne had to see the Company Doctor --across the river at Syriam. While going by boat across, I mentioned to her that my right elbow felt a little sore. On her advice I took the opportunity and showed it to the Doctor. He examined it and told me to seek the advice of a Dr. Edwards from W.H.O. as he was not sure of what it was. I made a few enquiries and was told about where he practised. I didn't know then that I was seeing the wrong Dr. Edwards. After a brief examination and without doing any tests he informed me that I had leprosy. He gave me some tablets which I had to take for about 3 years. I was also advised that I should visit the clinic every 3 months. I took the tablets for only a month and then never visited the doctor again.

In Perth, 20 years after I'd left the war, I still had these very itchy feet, which was really quite unbearable. I approached my GP, Dr. Metcalf, and told him the story about leprosy. He at once telephoned Sir Charles Gardiner Hospital and informed the Infectious Diseases Department. I was told to go there immediately. There was no waiting either at the reception desk or at the Doctor's. There were five Doctors who had a look at the arm. They took X-rays and blood samples.

'The verdict Mr. Stephenson,' they said, 'is that there is nothing wrong with you. You must have hurt your arm sometime in your life.' I remembered crawling on them with my rifle. I cannot believe that all these years I had lived with this verdict that I had leprosy, and had worried and wondered what indeed could happen to me. Finally they discovered that it was some medication I was taking that was causing this itchiness.

Daphne's mum knitted a lot of baby clothes for children, so she asked us to take it all to the St. Francis Convent and hand them over to the Mother Superior. The Nuns were in the Chapel when we got there. While waiting we saw some children with their Carers all dressed very sweetly. We wandered over and were greeted by the kids who kept calling us 'Mummy and Daddy'. Tears welled up in our eyes. We looked around and spoke to some of them who were about 2 or 3 years old.

Knitting leads to family joys
The Mother Superior was delighted with the knitted garments. On our way home Daphne said to me, 'You know I liked those children so much. It made me think. What if we adopted a child?' It was sort of telepathy. I too was thinking along those lines. I was extremely excited to hear Daphne ask. It was interesting that we both liked the same child. She was a baby and was baptized Patricia, by the same French priest, Fr. Boney. Apparently, the story is that, the child was given to him when her mother died while giving birth to her. When we approached the Mother Superior later to tell her of our decision, she was only too happy to agree. That's how our lovely Patricia became part of our family.

It was only then that we informed Daphne's mum that she was to get a grand daughter. It was a grand and colorful day when Patricia was brought home. I stayed on in the Insurance Company for about 2 years. Then with my experience of making contact with various Government officials I moved to a Japanese firm, doing the same type of work with fewer responsibilities but, on the same pay and bonuses. It was also there that I learned to fumigate ships without them having to unload their cargo just by using Methyl Bromide.

About 12 years later I left my job and so did Daphne hers. She had worked for IBM as their Head Secretary. We had accumulated quite a bit of money and decided to become farmers in Maymyo. With encouragement from the Government, we purchased 2 Massey Fergusson Tractors and a Hydraulic Trailer. We managed to get about 800 acres of land just outside Maymyo and began tiling and sowing wheat and after that maize, getting two crops a year. We were very successful in the first two years but when the Government nationalized the mills, things sadly got bad. The crops had to be sold to them at their offering price.

The Brothers from St. Albert's School and the priests and nuns we knew were our good friends. They were in and out of our house in Maymyo and told us to think about our future and that of the children. On one such occasion, Father O'Rourke (American) visited us and spent the day with us. He also advised us to get out of the country. They all felt we had a future in another country, not in the new Burma. We took their advice. Daphne went down to Rangoon and, through her brother, managed to get an interview with Mr. Johnston, the Councilor, in the Australian Embassy. He however wanted to see Patricia and me. We had our interview and went back to Maymyo to pack up and move to Rangoon while awaiting the results of the interview, which we were quite sure were positive.

Patricia, at that time, spoke mainly Burmese, having had to learn that as a compulsory subject in school. English was taught as the Second Language. Besides that she was always with the Nanny and other Burmese children and so her English was not very fluent. We therefore arranged for her to have English tuition, as we had decided to migrate.

In Rangoon we stayed with Daphne's brother Ted and his family, and waited for our interview results to come through. At the sixth month after the interview, after not hearing of our acceptance, we decided to go to England on the advice of my oldest sister in Sheffield. Having proved that we were of third generation English grandparents, the British Embassy issued us with our Citizenship Passport for Australia. We were quite pleased we had managed to work it out. We booked our passage by BOAC and had to wait 4 weeks for our departure.

My brother-in-law chanced to meet Mr. Johnston, the Councilor at the Australian Embassy, at the airport who asked him how we were enjoying Australia. Ted told him that we had not got the OK yet. Mr. Johnston was quite surprised and told my brother-in-law, 'They were one of our quickest acceptances. It only took a month to process them.' I was furious. Daphne said to me, 'Let's take the Permanent Resident visa stamped on our passport.'

Moving up or moving Down-under?

Meanwhile, I approached the girl at the Australian Embassy desk and told her I had come for my visa. She turned around and said, 'Who told you that you have been accepted?'

I said, 'Mr. Johnston.'

On hearing the name of Mr. Johnston she pulled out from the bottom of the drawer the authority of acceptance. I then went in and saw Mr. Johnston and managed to get a nine-month visa, also informed him that we were first going to England.

Trophy D'Souza

These girls were ripping off those who were desperate to leave, asking for large sums of money to fill their own pockets. This particular lady now lives in Perth. It would be worth a conversation with her at some point in time. It might be worth putting the fact on Facebook or YouTube. It might help migrants to be careful of the procedures that they need to keep tabs on.

It was Government Policy, in migration processing, that all goods had to be checked at one's residence two weeks before departure. The Bureau of Special Investigation, Customs and Immigration, carried out these inspections. Every item we had, of clothing or other goods, was stamped and returned to its proper box. All ten trunks had been sealed and taken to the Custom House for further examination, one week before we left.

Meanwhile, we had to get our papers checked by a five-man committee. The first man asked me if my daughter was adopted and of course I said, 'No.' Patricia was 8 years old at the time.

He then took Patricia aside and asked her in Burmese, 'Where is your Mother and Father?' and she pointed to us. My heart was in my mouth.

He then asked us to produce her Baptism Certificate, which I did. Our good friend Father Aseer had arranged that we have a Baptism Certificate showing she was the daughter of Charles and Daphne Stephenson. In Burma, there is no such thing as legal adoption. We were fortunate to have got away with that too.

Ted was looking through our Passports and noticed Patricia's name not on it. There again the men at the British Embassy knew she was adopted and had left out her name.

Daphne walked in to Mr. Constance's office (Councilor) and while crying explained the story also saying, 'How could we leave this child whom we have had since the time she was a baby?' Mr. Constance told her to come back on Monday and that she would be on the passport. On the weekend Mr. Constance visited the crèche and spoke to the Reverend Mother and that put everything in place.

Meanwhile we sold most of our jewelry, as we were not allowed to take it out. However, we purchased a Star Ruby and I hoped to take it out with us because after all it was our own hard- earned money that we wished to take with us. The Government allowed us only 75 GB Pounds for the family in foreign exchange.

On going to Customs House for the final examination of the boxes, I put the Ruby and some other bits into my handkerchief, inside my pocket, hoping to get a chance to take them with us. All the boxes were opened and thoroughly examined. When we were at the last box I managed to slip the contents from my pocket on the top of some clothing, put the lid down but was told not to lock the boxes as the Appraiser was on his way and might want to do his examination. My heart was close to skipping a heartbeat. I was really worried and kept talking to myself to remain calm. I sent the servant girl home, as I did not want her implicated. She went back and told Daphne all that was happening. We just had to rely on prayers and divine intervention. The Appraiser arrived but did not wish to open the boxes. That was indeed great relief to me and my wife. So, I locked the boxes and got out quickly before any change of mind. In those times and days even the gold chains around our necks had to be shortened to meet the required weight. Some people even had to give up their wedding rings.

Sojurning in England
We arrived in London on the 1st of May 1965. I went up to Sheffield by train and stayed with my sister on Barnsley Road. Daphne did not like the place and was in tears most of the time as we were practically squeezed into my sister' attic room. My younger brother Noel had some influence around and took us back to the Railway Station, fished out the ruby and instructed the staff to please send the boxes back to East Croydon. Within the week, we were back in Croydon. We both got jobs at once: Daphne got back to IBM Moorgate in London as a Secretary and I worked in a factory, perforating tapes for the US Navy. Because of my shift work we hardly had time for any companionship. Patricia went to school and came home when it was getting dark, at 3 o'clock in the afternoon and so we didn't have much time with her either. It was quite difficult for us moving away from a place with a big house on 4 acres of land (in Burma) and servants to do our on cooking and other household chores.

Daphne too didn't really have any idea about cooking, so it was a slog. But with the help of some Burmese friends and relations, she managed and learned. However, we were still not settled. The Manager of IBM informed Daphne that the company would finance us for a house. We went around looking for one but could not find any that we liked or could afford. One day in November, before we went out on our rounds searching for a house, we opened the thick velvet curtains and found the weather gloomy and terrible: it was rainy and windy, cold and dreary. Daphne sat on the bed with tears in her eyes and said. 'Charles, let's go to Australia!...I can't bear this anymore.' I told her that this indeed was the best news she could have given me.

In a friend's car, we shot off to the Australian Embassy and were told to just buy our tickets and go, as we already had our visas. In Burma we had paid a family passage to England and now they had reimbursed us the amount - 500 Pounds - which amount covered us by boat to Australia. At Southampton, we had a few problems with Australian Immigration, due to the 'White' Australian Policy. They could not believe we Asians were on this ship the 'Australis'.

Everyone boarding to migrate to Australia only paid 10 pounds. We being colored and born in another country had to pay the full fare, even though we were British Citizens. On board the 30,000-ton liner, at every staircase there were pamphlets of the 'White Australian Policy'. Daphne and I looked at one another and wondered 'What are we getting ourselves into?' However, we stuck it out even though we did not have that bit of extra money to spend on deck. We saw a little of Cairo and Athens on the way but while nearing Australian waters we all got quite seasick. Patricia though literally had a ball on the journey and also performed a Burmese Pye dance at one of the deck parties.

Reverend Father Foley (later Archbishop) migration Chaplain, met us at Fremantle. He knew that we were homesick and took us straight up to King's Park. What a lovely gesture it was. We stayed with friends from Burma and slept on the floor for 3 months. I took a job with 'Allpest' in Canning Highway and was given a car with its pest control gear and commenced my work. I fumigated two ships for them. I could not convince the authorities not to take the crew off the ship as is done in Japan, Burma and America. I did however fumigate a bakery to the annoyance of Mr. Moyle the Health Inspector of Perth. You should have seen the rats and cockroaches that were killed.

Beginning life again

I requested and was sent to Exmouth (a US Base) and was in-charge of spraying the foundations of the buildings before construction. I managed to get another two jobs on the weekends. All this income gave us a start in this lovely country. We bought a home in Nollamara and in 1967 joined the MLC Insurance 1968. I was the top salesman in the collectors Department and Superintendent in 1969. Patricia meanwhile, after winning the contest on the show 'Stars of the Future' while still in school at the age of 13, was for the next two years a regular on the program. On the weekends she would sing at Romano's Night Club for $30. Someone sent her name to Channel 9 in Melbourne for an Audition for 'Show Case'. She was accepted and I am proud to say that she got the Judge's second and the Viewers' first prize. She was also the first West Australian to sing in the Sydney opera House.

After ten years in Insurance and with the pressure building, I decided on something easier and got a job with 'Worths' and was a very successful Suit Salesman and became one of the Managers in Carousel. At the age of 60, with the kindness of the Australian Government and being a war veteran, I retired. I went to England for a holiday and while there had a Cardiac Infraction. I was happy to get back home to Australia safe and well.

This is a Lucky Country. 'Life was never meant to be easy' as stated by Mr. Malcolm Fraser. Not long after our arrival I remember a Labour Minister saying, 'Burmese migrants are living on the smell of an oily rag.' It was quite a rude remark. In his ignorance he did not realize that Australians now eat healthier food. Most Australians are now consuming varied and delicious menus of Asian meals.

Patricia married and has two children, a girl Simone and a boy Adam. Simone married an American and has two kids, a boy and a girl. Adam is studying in America. One can feel quite proud to see and know that many Burmese boys and girls have integrated and worked hard in this new country of ours. There have been some Burmese migrants serving in the Australian Forces and even in Vietnam. My story will tell you that our 'Anglo' loyalty is unquestionable.

Daphne and I now live in a Catholic Retirement Village (Castledare) in Wilson (in the Perth area in Western Australia). I carry out the Sacristan duties as an Acolyte in the Chapel also taking Communion to the sick. I'm writing this true story of my life because I want my story to be read by anyone who wants to know how we Anglos went through our paces, how we minorities survived our doses of discrimination, and how I survived a difficult childhood, a painful school-life and a challenging army career. At the end of my tale I feel relieved of a very heavy burden of facts and happenings that may have stayed hidden away from Daphne and from the rest of my family and friends for nearly sixty years. I think it was worth the wait because the story had to be explained properly in all its detail more for my family and friends than for any gain or redemption. My story is also the story of many unsung heroes,

Trophy D'Souza

men and women, who may not get their stories in print but who still deserve to be honored, admired and remembered.

The End

The Author

Trophy D'Souza writes for those who do not have a voice or who are not able to express themselves. He does his best to stand up for the underdog and does take up causes that need a hearing. He is aware that suffering often goes unanswered and that the stories of many people who suffer, or who are disadvantaged, get lost in an immense cover-up that leaders, rulers and managers skilfully and unabashedly manoeuvre. Trophy's contribution is perhaps a drop in the ocean but it is nevertheless a voice that can help make a difference.

Charles' story exposes the dysfunctional nature of some managers in education who instead of nurturing a precious little soul chose to lash out with their brute sense of righteousness. He didn't fare much better at home where a heartless father nearly smothered his free spirit in his childhood. His magnanimity in caring for his undeserving father shows the inner character of a noble soul. His life in the army brought him mixed fortunes in care, nurturing and fellowship but it strengthened him in his resolve to be a better human being. The Chindit ideals that he imbibed as part of his army program became integral to his dedication, commitment and service.

Trophy's first book (A Bumpy Ride), his third (Anastasia Redeemed) and his fourth (The Silence Beyond the Pain) also speak of dysfunctional situations, but generally those in religious settings. His second (The Singh Saga) shows more involvement with family situations though not in the same vein as in Charles' account. Charles' story is one of a kind: one that needs to be read to be appreciated and believed!

Guidance for Readers and Acknowledgements

*<u>The book</u> is really about Charles Stephenson and his story written for him by Trophy D'Souza. The settings of Burma and the background of World War II blend into the narrative that gives Readers a peep into history and into the experiences of an insider in the War. The Author has tried to keep as close as possible to the language and style of Charles in his diaries so that Readers can appreciate the anxieties and uncertainties of War experienced by him.

*<u>Places in Burma</u>: The Author has made every effort to locate many of the places as given in the maps. But it is really the descriptions, the anecdotes and the narratives that matter and so some places have not got mention either in the maps or even in the Glossary. It might be handy to refer to the maps whenever the narrative isn't all that clear.

*<u>Glossary</u>: This provides helpful guidance to Readers and in some ways acts as an Appendix to the main narrative. It is possible to enjoy the story without referring to the Glossary or the maps.

*<u>Army terminology</u> can be confusing, and even if the Author has done his best to explain them it is best to go with the 'narrative' rather than on try to unravel the complicated Army terms.

*<u>Three individuals</u> who have experience of writing and of critical evaluation have reviewed the book. They do not wish

to be singled out: ERM, FRG, TMT. They have either lived for short periods in Burma or who have experienced the War. They have assisted with valuable comments, historical data and other corrections, and with the proof-reading too.

*<u>Other individuals</u> also need to be mentioned: Mary Gilmore who assisted with data, suggestions and communications with the Editor/Author; Mrs Hilda Polglase who encouraged and inspired him in the first place to tell his story; Mrs Mary Skinner who typed the 1st draft from the recordings on the cassette; Mr Larry McIntosh, his son-in-law for the printouts and locations identified; Mr Godfrey Baronie, his nephew for his input, contributions and for the 2nd and 3rd drafts; Liz Torres who stepped in almost at the last moment to assist in the publishing process.

*<u>Currency</u> references: Generally the US $ is referred to as the point of reference. ($ & Cents)

*<u>This symbol</u> ° after a word or a phrase in the text indicates that there is an explanation for it in the Glossary at the end of the book.

GLOSSARY and NOTES

--**American Baptist**: a Christian denomination, based in America [USA].

--**Anawartha**: the beginnings of Buddhist thought and belief. Anawartha (1044-1077) was one of two rulers who patronized Buddhism and the Shwezigon Pagoda in Bagan° , where a tooth relic of the Buddha (donated by Sri Lanka) is enshrined. This pagoda, because of its style and importance, became the model on which many of the pagodas in Burma were built. It then eventually became a centre for Buddhist thought and philosophy as well.

-- **Anglican**: one of the Protestant denominations of Christians; England is the home of Anglicanism.

--**Anglo**: Anglo-Burmese and/or Anglo-Indian

--**Anglo-Burmese**: a person of mixed British and Burmese parentage, sometimes also called Anglo-Indian.

--**Anglo-Indian**: a person of mixed British and Indian parentage, a term that later took on legal significance.

--**Anna & Pice**: 4 Pice make an Anna. 16 Annas make a Rupee.

--**Apalon** Station: one of the stations on the death railway, built by its prisoners (POWs). Neeky was on the Thailand side and Apalon station was on the Burmese side

--**Arakanese**: This tribe in Burma forms the majority along the coastal region of present day Rakhine State. They constitute over 5.53% of Myanmar's total population. The Arakanese also live in the south eastern parts of Bangladesh. This group, known as the Marma people, have been living in that area since the Arakanese kingdom's control of the Chittagong region of Bangladesh. The Arakanese eventually spread as far north as Tripura in India.

--ARMY Terminology:

- **Army Artillery** Unit: corresponds to a Company in an Infantry Regiment
- **Army**: divided into Divisions
- **Army Hierarchy**: Lieutenant, Captain, Major, Colonel, Brigadier, General.....Field Marshal?
- **Artillery**: a branch of the army that uses large guns
- **Artillery Battery**: a unit of guns, mortars, rockets or missiles so grouped in order to facilitate better battlefield communication, command and control, as well as to provide dispersion for its constituent gunnery crews and their systems.
- **Battalion** = 3 Companies (i.e. app 72x3 = 216 soldiers) —usually split into 2 Columns (see Column)
- **Battery (soldiers)** = Field Battery is about the same as Artillery Battery.
- **Battery (equipment)** = 8 Field Guns
- **Brigade** = 3 Battalions (i.e. approx 216x3 = 648 soldiers) It is similar to a Regiment, & could have app 4 Battalions in it. Three Brigades make up a Division.
- **Column**: each Column had between 800 and 1000 men.
- **Column Battalion**: this was different: = 3 Platoons (i.e. approx 24x3 = 72 soldiers)
- **Company** = 3 Platoons (i.e. approx 24x3 = 72 soldiers)
- **Division** = 3 Brigades (i.e. approx 648x3 = 1944 soldiers)

-**Field Gun**: between 8 and 12 men were the crew to an average sized/type Field Gun.

-**Field Guns** used by the British Army: 18 Pounders, 25 Pounders

-**Field Marshal**: senior most official in the army, above a General.

-**Platoon** = 3 Sections (i.e. approx 8x3 = 24 soldiers)

-**Regiment**: about 800 men, commanded by a Colonel, divided into 2 Battalions or into 8 Companies.

-**Section** = 8 Soldiers

---<u>ABBREVIATIONS:</u>

-BAF	Burma Auxiliary Force
-BIC	British Intelligence Corps
-BMH	Burma Military Hospital
-BOAC	British Overseas Airways Corporation
-BOR	British Other Rank
-CO	Commanding Officer
-IO	Intelligence Officer
-MO	Medical Officer
-NCO	Non Commissioned Officer
-OC	Officer in Charge
-RAMC	Royal Army Military Corps
-RSM	Regimental Sergeant Major
-RTO	Regimental Transport Officer
-WACI	Women's Auxiliary Corp India

--**Aung Sang Suu Kyi**: Prominent woman in Burmese politics, who spent many years in detention under the Burmese Army. Her father, Aung San, who was an Army General, trying to build up the Burma Resistance Army, With the help of the Japanese (an Axis Power) was assassinated.

--**Bagan**: The capital from the 5th to 9th centuries. It is 26 sq miles; 118 miles South of Mandalay and 429 miles North of Yangon. It has temples of those eras.

--**Bangalore Torpedoes**: Type of field gun.

--**Batman**: an officer's personal attendant: in the British army.

--**Battery** was a unit of artillery belonging to the Brigade.

--**Bernard Shaw**: Irish-English writer, dramatist. His theory of man's insuperable powers to survive the odds stacked against him as explained also in his plays: *Man and Superman* and *Saint Joan*.

--**Bible**: the holy book of the Christians: consisting of 63 books: 39 known as the Old Testament, and 24 called the New Testament. 4 of the New Testament books are the 'Gospel' books by writers Mathew, Mark, Luke and John.

--**Black Cat** Division: [see 17th Division]

--**Block**: a tactical military manoeuvre, using men and ammunition, to stop an enemy from advancing or attacking.

--**Broadway Airfield:** located 35 miles east-north-east of Indaw°, which itself had a landing strip. It was a code name for one of the four landing points around Indaw, named by Wingate°. Piccadilly was one of the others. Indaw was selected because it was uninhabited. It was also flat ground which was ideal for building an airstrip in a short period of time, and most important of all was the fact that there was water nearby.

--**Brothers**: members of Catholic Religious Orders, who took vows of poverty, chastity and obedience, and lived in Communities and took up social projects like teaching, nursing and social work. De La Salle° was one such Order.

--**Buddhism** [Buddhist Monks]: Buddhism is the main religion in Burma. Buddhist monks play a significant part in social life even if the Army still dominates the scene. Pali is the language of worship in Buddhism.

--**Burma**: The Author chose to use this older name instead of Myanmar, the new name for Burma. In 1989, the political leaders of the country changed it. In 'Burmese', the national language, Burma is spelt as 'Myanmar'. Burma is located in South East Asia and is also known as the Land of Pagodas. There are many pagodas and Buddhist shrines across the country. Burma is also naturally surrounded by mountains on its three sides.

--**Burman**: The original settlers of the land, who form about two-thirds of the population, still influence social and political life. Research has shown that the Burmans are related by a common ancestry in the far north on the one hand to the Tibetans and on the other to the far-spread Lolos of South-Western China, and the language test shows that the relationship can be traced up through a host of allied tribes occupying the country that now separates the three peoples. It must have been somewhere in the eastern portion of the Central Asian table land that the Tibeto-Burman race acquired an identity of its own and that it was from this region that, over many centuries, it sent its off-shoots out along the valleys and hill ridges into Burma and Indo-China. These people harmoniously merged with the people who were previously living on the land, and gradually took on the name 'Burman'.

--**Calcutta**: A strategic point for the British in Bengal, which is the older version for the new name, Kolkata.

--**Catholic**: one belonging to the largest group of Christians in the world. The Pope in Rome is the head.

--**Chin**: a tribe in Burma. The name 'Chin' is disputed. The British used 'Chin-Kuki-Mizo' to group the Kukish language speaking people, and the Government of India inherited this. Christian Missionaries chose to use 'Chin' to christen those on the Burmese side and 'Kuki' on the Indian side of the border. Chin nationalist leaders in Burma's Chin State popularized the term 'Chin' following Burma's independence from Britain. Of the Western Tibeto-Burmans the Chins or Kukis were probably the first arrivals in Burma. In the distant past they must have appeared on the Irrawaddy-Brahmaputra watershed, continued their southerly journey along the western edge of the Province, and then worked their way down to the southern limits of the hilly country on the sea-board of the Bay of Bengal.

--**Chindit**: The name given to the soldiers in his Regiment by British Commander General Charles Wingate after the mythical griffin, the Chinthe –the half lion and half eagle guardian of the Burmese Temples. The Chindits were thelargest of the allied Special Forces of the 2nd World War. They were formed and lead by Major General Orde Wingate DSO. The Chindits operated deep behind enemy lines in North Burma in the War against Japan. For many months they lived in and fought the enemy in the jungles of Japanese occupied Burma, totally relying on airdrops for their supplies. There were two Chindits expeditions into Burma, the first in February 1943 Operation Longcloth, consisted of a force of 3,000 men who marched over 1,000 miles during the campaign. The second expedition, Operation Thursday, in March 1944 was on a much larger scale. It was the second largest airborne invasion of the war and consisted of a force of 20,000 British and Commonwealth soldiers with air support provided by the

1st Air Commando USAAF. Tragically their leader, General Wingate, was killed a few weeks after the launch of Operation Thursday. The Chindits were very much an International Force, which included British, Burma Rifles, Hong Kong Volunteers, Gurkhas and West African Serviceman. The R.A.F. and First Air Commando , U.S.A.A.F. provided air support.

--**Chindwin**, River: (see Map): it flows through the Kabaw° valley, in central Burma.

--**Chinese**: the Chinese fighting on the side of the Allies in World War II were from 'Nationalist China', then based off today's mainland China. The situation changed soon after the War.

--**Column**: each column had approximately 800 to 1000 men but due to heavy casualties and shortage of men two columns often merged to became one

--**Darwin**, Charles: anthropologist whose theories on Evolution influenced modern thinking.

--**David & Goliath**: the Bible (1 Sam, 17:50) story: where David a shepherd boy overcomes Goliath the Philistine, with a stone thrown from his sling.

--**De La Mare**, Walter: English poet, wrote 'The Listeners'. The first line, 'Is there anyone there?' which is repeated in the poem, creates a haunting sense of disbelief and mystery.

--**De La Salle**: A Catholic Religious Order of men (Brothers not priests), who run schools/colleges across the world.

--**Division**: 17th Division: (Black Cats) were based in several parts of Burma. They were known as the Black Cat Division because of the shoulder badge they wore. They operated from India into Burma. They were stationed in the Moulmein area. Charles was attached to them.

--**Fireman**: one in the hierarchy of jobs in the 'Loco Department' (Engine Dept) of the Railways.

--**Furlough:** permission to leave army duties for a short period of time.

--**Good Samaritan**: story in the Bible (Gospel) which speaks of a lower 'class' person stopping to save an unknown wounded traveller while others apparently higher placed in society passed by without offering help.

--**Gospel**: the 4 books (of the 24) in the New Testament (see Bible) written by Mathew, Mark, Luke and John.

--**Gurkhas:** They were a Battalion on their own and were selected to be part of Special Force. They were recruited directly from Nepal.

--**Hailakandi**: a town in Assam (India) bordering the Indian state of Mizoram and Bangladesh, with reserved forests in the vicinity. The people speak the Bengali language.

--**Henu**: on the railway link, with Henu Hill alongside. Henu was north of Mawlu & app 120 km south of Mogaung and at least 970 km north of Rangoon, with a Dakota strip just west of the town.

--**Hindi**: one of the 2 official languages of India, used by around 400 million people worldwide & spoken by about 40% of India's population . It is the 6th most spoken language in the world.

--**Htameins**: girls' dresses, used in Burma.

--**Hukaung** valley: (also spelt Hukawng) is in the northern most part of Burma, in the Myitkyina° district of the Kachin° state.(see Maps)

--**Imphal**: the capital of Manipur, a state in eastern India.

--**Indaw** airfield: one of 2 air strips (with Myitkyina) in the northern part of Burma, near Indaw lake.

--**Inle Lake**: 13.5 Miles long and 7 miles wide. Known for its floating pagodas, crafts work ships and its log rafters.

--**Kabaw** valley: a highland valley in northern Burma, home to a number of ethnic tribes, including the Mizo, who form a state in neighbouring India called Mizoram. (see Maps).

--**Kachin**: The Kachin people are a group of ethnic groups who largely inhabit the Kachin Hills in northern Burma's Kachin State and the neighbouring areas of China and India. More than half of the Kachin people identify themselves as Christians - while a significant minority follow Buddhism and some also adhere to animism. Kachin state is also known as the land of jades and gold.

--**Kalaw**: a small town in Burma, east of Thazi, north of Rangoon.

--**Kamout**: pointed hat with a broad rim, worn by the buffalo-cart drivers

--**Karen**: refers to a number of Sino-Tibetan language speaking ethnic groups which reside primarily in Karen State in southern and southeastern Burma. The Karen people make up approximately 7 percent of the total 5 million population of Burma. Large numbers of Karens have migrated to Thailand, settled on the Thai–Karen border.

There are Karens also in the USA and in Sweden.

--**Kukri**: (also 'Khukuri)' is a Nepalese knife with a slight inwardly curved blade, used as a weapon and as a tool: a basic utility knife of Nepalese. Gurkha troops are issued a kukri. The Chindits were also trained in Kukri skills.

--**Kyat**: Burmese currency: 5 Kyats = 1 US$ --during the period of World War II.

--**Lahore:** at the time of the War it was in India. It is now a city in Pakistan.

--**Lodore**: The Cataract of Lodore: poem by Robert Southey, English Poet.

--**Loihinche**: South East of Mogaung, around app 1100 km east of Rangoon.

--**Lotus-eaters**: poem by English poet, Alfred Tennyson. He is affected by the loss of a friend, and seems to take refuge away from the harsh realities of life, like the people in the poem who ate the Lotus and were transported into an 'altered state' somewhat 'isolated from the world.

--**Malwagon**: Situated 6 miles east of Rangoon. It housed employees of the Burma Railways.

--**Mandalay**: Burma's second largest city; in the central highlands, north of Rangoon, the capital.

--**Mawlu**: a small town on the Mandalay-Myitkyina railway, about fifty miles south west of Broadway.

--**Maymyo**: a large town in north-east of Burma, in the Shan Plateau; with a cool climate (like Darjeeling in India)

--**Meiktila**: An area (part of a district) in upper Burma

--**Mergui:** A town on the Tenassarim° coast of Burma

--**Merill Mauraders**: were the Americans who were in the South of Myitkyina° and were there to aid
General Stilwell who was advancing from the North

--**Methodist**: one of the Christian denominations based in England.

--**Mile** = approx 1x 1.609 km: a British measure for distance.

--**Mindon** [King of Burma]: He ruled from 1858 to 1878. The British annexed lower Burma during his reign, and later annexed the rest of Burma under the rule of his brother, Pagan. He was a King loved by his people.

--**Mogaung**: on the Mogaung river and on the Mandalay-Myitkyina railway link, app 50 km south west of Myitkyina°. It is in the Kachin° state.

--**Mohinyin**: on the railway link north of Indaw° and Mawlu°, and directly west of Broadway°, a landing point.

--**Mon**: tribal people in Burma with their own dialect/language.

--**Mote phet thoke**: a Burmese sweet.

--**Moulmein**: (also spelt Mawlamyine -in south Burma) is the fourth largest city of Burma, situated 300 km south east of Yangon and 70 km south of Thaton, at the mouth of Thanlwin river. It is in the strip of Burma near (southeast of) Yangon (Rangoon) that splits and then tapers down towards Thailand. It was a strategic point in WWar2.

--**Mudon** Lakes: situated app 30 km south of Moulmein°, is the first major town south of Moulmein, on the way to Thanbyuzayat°. During World War II Thanbyuzayat was the western terminus of the Thailand-Burma Railway linking up with the pre-war coastal railway between Ye and Rangoon. Thanbyuzayat was also the site of

a Japanese Prisoner of war camp for the prisoners who worked on building the railway. Over 3,000 Allied servicemen are buried in the Thanbyuzayat War Cemetery

--**Mustang**: a fighter plane used by the British army.

--**Myanmar**: the new name for Burma. (See Burma)

--**Myingyan**: is a city & district in the Mandalay Division of central Burma. Earlier it was a district in the

the Meiktila Division of Upper Burma: to the north of Rangoon, to the south of Mandalay, west of Thazi. The city had a population of 123,700. It lies in the valley of the Ayeyarwady River, on the east bank of the river. The area around the town is flat. The most noticeable feature is Popa Hill, an extinct volcano, to the south-east. There are no forests, but a great deal of low scrubland. Myingyan is the head of the branch railway to Thazi and the main line between Rangoon and Mandalay. The town got notoriety for its infamous prison and detention centre for Burma's political prisoners from early 1990s' to October 1999 when the International Committee for Red Cross (ICRC) stopped the abuses.

--**Myitkyina**: The capital of Kachin State in the north of Burma, 1480 km (920 mi) from Rangoon, & 785 km from Mandalay. In Burmese it means 'near the big river'. It is on the west bank of the River Ayeyarwady, It is the northernmost river port and railway terminus in Burma. The city is served by a little Airport that was strategically important for the airlift of soldiers and civilians to India.

--**Neeky**: see Apalon

--**Pagoda**: A pagoda is commonly a Buddhist structure where sacred relics could be kept and venerated, or it could be a point at which religious worship is organized also in non-Buddhist beliefs. A pagoda is often used to mean stupa or temple, with a series of superimposed spires. In the book it refers to a structure used in Buddhism.

--**Pali**: the language used in Buddhism and Buddhist scriptures. It was the Vernacular language of northern India in the Buddha's time, so it is the original language for the Buddhist texts, including the canon of Buddhist writings, the Pali Canon, the basic Buddhist Scriptures.

--**Pazaungdaung**: a township located in the south eastern part of Yangon.(Also spelt as Pazundaung).

--**Phongyi**: Buddhist monk.

--**Phongyi Kyaung**: Burmese/Buddhist schools where basic education was given to children.

--**Prodigal Son**: Bible (Gospel) story: the younger of 2 sons takes his inheritance and blows it all away, and has to survive literally by eating the husks given to the pigs he has to feed. He decides to return to his father to work for him, but his father orders a banquet to welcome him back, and treats him with all the affection of a father.

--**Pyuntaza**: A small railway station on the Mandalay to Rangoon main route.

--**Railway Jobs** Hierarchy (Loco Department): Fireman, Shunter, Driver, Loco Foreman, Loco Inspector.

--**Rangoon**: the capital of Burma, in the south touching the sea; also spelt and known as Yangon today.

--**Rupee**: currency of India. (16 Annas made a Rupee.) Today 100 Paisa make a Rupee.

--**Samaw**: a place in the Mohnyin area, in the Kachin state.

--**Sarong**: a loose garment wrapped around the waist, reaching down to the feet, used in Burma.

--**Shewbo** airport: It is a town on the Bagan° - Mandalay railway route.

--**Shunter**: one in the hierarchy of jobs in the 'Loco Department' (Engine Dept) of the Railways.

--**Special Forces**: There's a long history behind such 'forces'. The British commandos were the first of such groups formed under Winston Churchill in 1940. The first modern Special Force was the SAS formed in 1941. In the Burma Campaign, the Chindits, whose long range penetration groups were trained to operate from bases deep behind Japanese lines, contained commandos (King's Regiment (Liverpool), 142 Commando Company) and Gurkhas. Their jungle expertise, which would play an important part in many British special forces operations post war, was learned at a great cost in lives in the jungles of Burma fighting the Japanese.

--**Staffords**: A reference to the 1st Battalion South Staffordshire Regiment

--**Tenasserim**: narrow *coastal* region, in SE Burma, bordering Thailand on the east and the Andamans on the west.

--**Tennyson,** Alfred: English poet wrote 'The Charge of the Light Brigade' about a whole bunch of soldiers who had to ride into a situation that they all knew was an Order that had gone wrong. Their words in the poem, 'Ours but to do and die' have rung out across the ages to army leaders whose poor decisions lead to loss of lives.

--**Thanbyuzayat**: a town in the Mon State of south eastern Burma. It is about 64 km south of Moulmein° and 24 kilometres south-east of Kyaikkami. . During World War II Thanbyuzayat was the western terminus of the Thailand-Burma Railway linking up with the pre-war coastal railway between Ye and Rangoon. Thanbyuzayat was also the site of a Japanese Prisoner of War camp for prisoners who worked on building the railway. Over 3000 Allied servicemen are buried in the Thanbyuzayat War Cemetery.

--**Thazi**: a small town in Burma, north of Rangoon, the capital, and north west of Henu, Mawlu and White City.

--**Toungyi**: a small town in Burma, east of Thazi, north of Rangoon; it had a small landing strip.

--**Untouchable**: a group of people, in traditional Indian society, also called Dalits, or officially 'Scheduled Caste'. They were also formerly known as Harijans, in traditional Indian society. These distinctions, where these groups were considered outside the caste system of Hindu groups in India, do not officially exist today, but they did at the time the events of this narrative took place.

--**VC**: Victoria Cross –an Army Award, in the British Army, given for exceptional bravery.

--**Warrant:** a release or travel Order issued by the Army usable/exchangeable in Civilian circles/organizations. Warrants could only be used for transportation on trains.

--**Wingate**, Charles: (see Chindit)

--**Wordsworth**, William: English poet who wrote the sonnet, *Upon Westminster Bridge*. The first line starts off with the wonderful scene he beholds, 'Earth has not anything to show more fair'.

--**Yenangyaung**: the town with oil fields and the oil refinery, on the River Irrawaddy, in south central Burma.

--**Zero**: a fighter plane used by the Japanese.

Map 1 – Burma – The Country

Lightning Source UK Ltd.
Milton Keynes UK
UKHW011820260522
403577UK00001B/313